I WANTED HIM TO DIE, DAN.
I NEVER FELT THAT BEFORE.
WHAT'S WRONG WITH ME?

THE VIPER'S NEST

THE 39 CLUES

PETER LERANGIS

SCHOLASTIC INC.

NEW YORK TORONTO LONDON AUCKLAND
SYDNEY MEXICO CITY NEW DELHI HONG KONG

For the wonderful readers, librarians,
and teachers I have met, and will meet,
through this series

—P.L.

Library of Congress Control Number: 2009933347

ISBN: 978-0-545-06047-9

10 9 8 7 6 5 4 3 2 1   10 11 12 13 14

Book design and illustration by SJI Associates, Inc.

First edition, February 2010

Printed in China 62

Scholastic US: 557 Broadway • New York, NY 10012
Scholastic Canada: 604 King Street West • Toronto, ON M5V 1E1
Scholastic New Zealand Limited: Private Bag 94407 • Greenmount, Manukau 2141
Scholastic UK Ltd.: Euston House • 24 Eversholt Street • London NW1 1DB

CHAPTER 1

Amy Cahill didn't believe in omens. But black snow was falling, the earth was rumbling beneath her feet, her brother was meowing, and her uncle Alistair was prancing on the beach in pink pajamas.

She had to admit, the signs were not promising.

"Ahoy, Nellie!" Alistair shouted across the Java Sea, his hands cupped to his mouth. "Rescue us, dear girl!"

Amy wiped a dark flake from her cheek. *Ash.*

Could it be left over from the fire last night?

Don't think of that. Not now.

Out at sea, a distant engine noise grew louder. On a small launch, speeding toward the tiny Indonesian island where they were stranded, was Amy and Dan's au pair, Nellie Gomez. In the eerie morning darkness, sky and water merged into a blue-gray wall, and she seemed to be floating in midair.

"Mrrrrrrrrrrp!" Dan wailed.

"What are you doing?" Amy asked.

"Imitating an Egyptian Mau." Dan gave Amy an exasperated look, as if what he had just said made perfect sense. "Saladin hates the water. If he hears another Mau, maybe he'll come on deck with Nellie — and we'll see him at least! Don't you miss him?"

Amy sighed. "I do. But after last night . . . I mean, I love Saladin, too, Dan, but honestly I haven't thought too much about him."

She heard a distant rumble of thunder. As she glanced out to sea, her eyes stung. A tear washed a gray line down her cheek. How could a fire from last night still produce so much ash? It was only one building. A place where she and Dan and Alistair would have become charcoal if it weren't for . . .

Don't think of her. Think about normal things. Peanut butter. Homework. TV. Saladin.

But images from last night were racing through her mind. The flames licking up the wall . . . Dan's expression, like a frightened toddler . . . Alistair shouting to them . . . the call from out the window, from the last person they'd wanted to see . . . the woman who had almost murdered them in Russia.

You thought she was trying to burn you alive last night. But she wasn't. It wasn't Irina.

Isabel Kabra had done it. She had burned down their house in Massachusetts all those years ago, and Dan and Amy's parents hadn't been able to escape. Now Isabel was finishing the job. She was a murderer. A Lucian killing machine in pearls and perfume.

Until last night, Isabel had been one of the two people Amy had feared most.

The other was the blond woman who had called up to them from below the ledge.

Yesterday, if you'd asked Amy to list the *Predictions Least Likely Ever to Come True in a Million Years,* right up there with *The world will turn into cheese* and *My brother Dan will say he loves me,* would have been this:

Irina Spasky will sacrifice herself — for us.

But Irina had leaped to the roof on a pole, into the flames. She had held that pole in front of their window so they could slide to safety. Then she had disappeared into the fire before Amy's eyes. Why?

How could a person change so much?

"Earth to Amy," Dan said. "Dude, can you hear what Nellie's saying?"

Stop. Thinking.

Amy's thoughts blew away into the smoky air. Out at sea, Nellie was waving frantically. Behind her, the sky was dark with ominous low clouds.

"The dear girl looks frightened," Alistair said.

"There's a storm coming," Amy said.

"Maybe she just noticed your pjs, Uncle Alistair," Dan suggested. "They *are* kind of scary."

Alistair glanced down. His silken sleepwear was tattered and sooty from the previous night's fire. "Oh, dear, would you pardon me while I change?"

Now Nellie was gesturing to something behind her, toward an island called Rakata. Amy stiffened. In 1883, the Krakatau volcano had erupted there, one of the worst natural disasters in recorded history.

Amy remembered the words of the motorboat skipper who had taken them here.

Not good today . . . very active.

She felt the ash on her cheek and suddenly it made sense. She held out her blackened fingertips toward her brother. It wasn't only the storm Nellie was worried about. "I — I think she's trying to tell us something about the volcano," Amy said.

Dan's eyes lit up. "Whoa. Are we going to be like Pompeii? Like, *hmm-hmm,* here we are, cleaning the kitchen — whoa, *zap!* — lavafied!"

"This is no joke," Amy said. "For your information, the last time the volcano blew, there were tidal waves all over the South Seas. Thirty-six thousand people died."

Dan took a deep breath. "Okay, Amy, let's chill. Nellie's almost here. In a few moments we'll be riding away, cuddling Saladin, everything situation normal. . . ."

"We have no lead, Dan," Amy said. "Even if we make it out of here, where do we go — back to Boston, so Social Services will take us to Aunt Beatrice?"

Dan glanced over toward where Alistair had disappeared. "I bet he knows where to go next."

"Great. After Alistair freshens up, we'll ask him," Amy said. "Do we have a lie detector handy? And where is he, anyway?"

As far as Amy was concerned, Alistair was the Whac-A-Mole of reliability. One minute he'd pop up in your life as protector and best friend. The next minute he'd betray you, and you wanted to bonk him down again.

Where had he gone to change clothes? Did he have a secret hiding place here? Was he going to vanish now, the way he had after the cave-in in Seoul?

The Ekaterinas had been on the Clues search for years. So had the other Cahill branches—the Tomas, the Lucians, and the Janus—all with money, experience, and the willingness to kill. The odds were so on their side. Grandmother Grace's will had raised the stakes by inviting handpicked Cahills to join a bizarre hunt to find 39 Clues that would lead to the greatest power ever known. But the will had given an out, too. Amy and Dan could have taken a million dollars each and forgotten about the hunt.

That choice would have been *normal*.

But Grace wanted them to find the Clues. And Amy couldn't imagine not doing what Grace wanted. Dan couldn't imagine not finding the greatest power ever known. Then there was the part about tracking hints left by famous ancestors, like Mozart and Ben Franklin. So here they were, four continents and six Clues later: a fourteen-year-old girl, her eleven-year-old brother, and an au pair whose main espionage training had involved downloading punk tunes and mastering tattoo pain—that is, unless she was really a master spy.

In the 39 Clues search, Abnormal was the new Normal.

Once again, Nellie's voice pierced the air. She was closer now, the launch's engine noise softening as it prepared to dock. Now her cry was crystal clear.

"POLICE!" She gestured over her shoulder. "POLICE!"

"They're going to arrest the volcano?" Dan asked.

"Come on!" Amy said, grabbing her brother's arm and heading toward Alistair. "A house burned down, Dan — and somebody died! Police investigate stuff like that. *Uncle Alistair! Nellie's being followed by the cops!*"

Alistair emerged from the nearby woods in a crisply pressed gray silk suit, his yellow shirt bright and clean, his bowler hat tilted just so. His face fell as he heard Nellie's cry. "Isabel . . ." he murmured. "She must have told the police we're to blame. That's her modus operandi."

Dan sighed. "You know, I follow you just fine and then *bam!* You stick in the vocabulary words."

Alistair gently placed the tip of his cane on Dan's foot, pinning him in place. He leaned into his nephew. "I know what you are doing. You believe that humor will lighten our load. But some things do not have a lighter side — like being thrown in jail in Jakarta. Because that, young man, is where we are all headed."

CHAPTER 2

"Rock star do not jump!" The launch was cutting sharply, its skipper calling out a phrase that bore no relationship to the English language as Amy knew it.

"Rock star in a hurry!" Nellie replied, one foot on the boat's gunwale. As the skipper docked next to a beat-up old fishing boat, Nellie tumbled out onto the soggy planks. She was dressed in a black jeans vest, shorts, striped knee socks, laceless red Converse, and a Mr. Bill T-shirt. Her spiky two-toned hair lay flat, making her head look from a distance like a wet skunk. As she ran to Dan and Amy, Saladin slinked along behind her. "Oh, my God, you guys!" Nellie cried out. "You're okay! I am *so happy* to see you!"

"Saladin!" Dan cried out, running toward the Mau.

"Saladin? What am I, chopped liver?" Nellie scooped both Dan and Saladin into a big hug as she walked. "Okay, listen up, dudes. We have to book. Yesterday, when I find you guys are, like, AWOL? I, like, freak. Yelling at everybody—*where are they, why did you let them leave*—the hotel people are, like, *whaaaa?* Anyway,

I pack up all your stuff, figuring I may never see the place again, and down in the lobby I find my man Arif. I'm, like, *help me,* and he takes all our stuff to this launch—and then we're halfway across the sea when Arif gets this radio message, and he's all excited, but I don't know what he's saying until he's, like, 'POLICE!' in English. And we see these cop cars and somebody's getting a big old boat, so we're, like, sayonara, only in Indonesian, and we tool out into this boat-traffic jam to try to lose them, and I'm hearing these radio reports that are half English—there's been a fire and somebody's dead, yada yada, and I'm totally wigging out—*Why did you do that? Why did you and your sister leave me in the hotel without even a note?*"

"Sorry," Dan began. "But you were sleeping—"

He glanced quickly at Amy. All their lives they had been able to communicate so much with just a look, and Amy silently gave him everything she could:

. . . and also, Nellie, we saw that you were receiving coded e-mails from someone . . .

. . . and back in Russia you also got a voicemail that said "Call in for a status report" . . .

. . . plus, you just happen to be able to fly a plane . . .

. . . and we hate to be paranoid, but one thing we learned on this clue hunt is "Trust no one."

"Dang! Do they do this in front of you, too, Al?" Nellie said, throwing Dan and Amy each a huge back-pack. "Mind-melding?"

Alistair looked flummoxed. "Do they . . . pardon?"

Nellie handed Saladin's cat carrier to Arif. She took Alistair's and Arif's arms and headed for the woods. "Don't mind us, kiddos. We're just going to hide in the trees. You can send us mental tweets from jail. Just include an explanation about why you betrayed your loyal babysitter."

"Wait, we're coming!" Dan said, donning his backpack as he ran after her. "And you're an *au pair*!"

As they neared the woods, Amy glimpsed the smoldering remains of the house. She turned away, not wanting to see. Not wanting to think about Irina.

Irina's visit to the island would not be round-trip.

The thought made Amy stop in her tracks. "Why don't we use Irina's fishing boat?" she called out. "The police won't recognize it."

"Far too small," Alistair said. "And I was the one who arrived on that boat, not Irina."

"Then how—" Dan said. "Uncle Alistair, is there another dock on this island?"

"Well, now that you mention it . . ." Alistair stopped, catching his breath. "Many years ago I found the remnants of a small sailing vessel in a tiny cove to the north. Why do you ask?"

"We may find our escape vessel there!" Amy blurted out. "If Irina didn't dock here, she may have pulled into that cove!"

"Brilliant, dear girl!" Alistair said.

"I was the one who thought of it," Dan grumbled.

Pulling free of Nellie, Alistair pointed his cane

confidently toward a distant tree. "Do you see that yellow mark high on the tree? It's a trail blaze. If we follow the trees marked in yellow, we will reach the cove. But the marks are quite faded, so we must proceed carefully. I shall bushwhack." He removed his jacket, placing it over his left arm, then held the arm out to Nellie. "Would you give me some support, dear girl?"

Nellie held on firmly to Alistair's jacket-draped arm. Alistair was walking fast, whacking at vines and branches with his cane. Arif followed behind, muttering. Before long, the contents of one of Alistair's jacket pockets began to spill.

"You're dropping things!" Dan scooped up a comb, mints, a handkerchief, and a small blue felt pouch.

The pouch had Russian writing on it.

"Whoa . . . is this Irina's?" Dan reached in and lifted out a vial of bluish liquid.

Alistair turned, mopping his brow with his sleeve. "Er, well, I saw something on the ground last night. Outside the house. I wasn't sure what it was, so . . ."

Irina's poisons, Amy thought.

Alistair took the pouch and walked away, tucking it into his pocket. He was so calm. So logical.

But . . . she died. These were her things. This is stealing.

Amy looked at Dan, but he was already running ahead, following the trail marks.

"*Dan?*" Nellie yelled. "*Yo, Indiana Jones, sound off so we know you're alive!*"

They stopped. A few seconds of tense silence were followed by a shriek.

"AAAAAAGGHHHH! SNAKES! GET OFF ME!"

Amy raced ahead. Her ankle caught on a rain-slickened vine and she tumbled over a bush and down a steep, sandy decline.

She landed in mud at the bottom, stopped by Dan's filthy Converse sneakers. He loomed above her, grinning, leaning against the prow of a large, two-level motorboat. "Found it first."

Amy scrambled to her feet. "I thought you were being attacked!"

"That was my Indy imitation. Good, huh?"

Amy smiled and then shoved Dan backward into the water. "That," she said, "was my Darth Vader."

CHAPTER 3

Standing at the rail, Dan Cahill looked over the roiling sea and thought: *He who is responsible for the fate of the world does not lose his lunch.*

He held tight, feeling like the time Aunt Beatrice had let him ride the Whirl-a-Cup after three helpings of French fries. The results weren't pretty.

The boat lurched on giant swells. The rain had let up, but that just made the volcanic ash worse. Between the ash and fog, Dan couldn't see the island where last night he and Amy almost became roast sibling stew. Arif had evaded the police by finding a channel behind the island. After circling south, he was now heading back to Jakarta. Well, *bouncing* back was more like it. The trip would take three hours. Which meant three hours of Radio Silence between Dan and his sister. Amy was mad at him.

He who is responsible for the fate of the world does not think about his sister while trying not to lose his lunch.

Usually, you could count to ten and Amy would start jabbering about some fascinating topic like the growth rate of flax in Uruguay. But this anger was different.

Sticky. Amy was mad at everybody—Alistair, Nellie, him.

Not that he blamed her. Everything was confusing, and confusion made Amy mad. Even their motto—*Trust no one*—couldn't be trusted. Irina was bad, then good. Nellie was good, then (maybe) bad. Alistair was in a class by himself. Plus, they didn't know where they were going next. And the ride was nauseating.

Take deep breaths. Think cheerful. Think funny.

A lot of help that strategy had been. No one was laughing at his jokes. But jokes were the only way to get relief from yesterday. From the memory of Irina.

He couldn't stop hearing her last words— *"Everything is up to you and Dan. Go!"* —or seeing her face. She was reaching up from under the sea, staring down from the storm clouds, crying on the wind.

Tickling his ankle.

"GAHH!" Dan gasped, jumping away.

"Mrrp?" said Saladin, looking as confused as he felt.

"Didn't mean to scare you, little guy," Dan said, lifting the Mau into his arms. He felt Saladin's heart beat against his own chest. "How do you do it? How do you make me feel so much better? I try to make everyone feel good, and I just get them mad. With you, it's like, hey, everything's situation normal."

Dan smiled. *Situation normal* was his dad's expression—one of the few things he remembered.

"Dude, I have someone I want you to meet," Dan said. He reached into his pocket and took out his father's old Australian passport. It had a faint musty, sweet smell. Dan imagined the smell was his dad's cologne, but Amy claimed it was just passport paper. Flipping open the blue cover, he looked at the photo and the fake name beneath: ROGER NUDELMAN. Dad had hidden his identity, probably to deceive rivals in the hunt. But the goofiness of the name always made Dan smile.

"Say hi, Rog!" he said softly. "He was a jokester, too, Saladin—I know it. Like me. Family tradition."

The boat lifted sharply up on a wave and then slapped down. Rain was beginning to fall again, so Dan quickly slipped the passport back into his pocket.

With a crack of thunder, the skies emptied hard. Dan cowered. Saladin jumped away and scampered toward a small glassed-in cabin. Dan followed, the rain so thick he could barely breathe.

"Ya, saya mendengar mereka—" Inside, the skipper, Arif, was shouting into a cell phone while at the wheel. He spun around suddenly. "No come in!"

"Um, rain?" Dan gestured outside. "Wet?" He shook his head, spraying water on the floor. "Towels?"

Arif muttered something into the phone in Indonesian, then pointed toward a hinged wooden chest that ran the length of the cabin's back wall.

Saladin was already scratching at something in the space between the chest and the wall. He managed to slide out a small oval-shaped tin. A rancid, fishy smell wafted upward and Dan felt his stomach lurch. As Saladin eagerly began licking out the slimy black contents, Dan noticed the tin's label: GENUINE RUSSIAN SEVRUGA CAVIAR.

Irina's snack.

Why did Russians like such disgusting food?

Breathe. In. Out.

You will not get sick.

Dan opened the chest and found a stack of white towels, along with ropes, blankets, and notebooks. As he pulled out a towel, he stopped cold.

Next to the stack was a leather shoulder bag engraved with the letters INS.

Irina N. Spasky.

Dan pulled it out and quietly shut the top.

The door to the cabin flew open, startling Arif. Amy barged in, soaked and angry looking. "There you are! I thought you'd hurled too many chunks and fallen off the edge of the boat."

Glancing at Arif, Dan tucked the shoulder bag under his arm. He pulled Amy outside to a rain-sheltering overhang. "Before you say anything that makes me feel even more special, look at this," Dan said.

Amy gasped when she saw the bag. "It's Irina's!"

Dan opened it and riffled through the contents—some makeup, a telescope shaped like a lipstick container, some suspicious-looking vials, a leather notebook . . .

"What's this?" Amy said, pulling out a thin leather wallet. Tucked inside was a stack of rubber-banded cards. Quickly, she unwrapped the bands and thumbed through. The top card made her flinch — a copy of her own United States Social Security card.

Under it were copies of Ian's and Natalie's school IDs, an ID card for each Holt, a Burrit-Oh! business card with a photo of a much-younger Alistair. . . . "Dan, this is scary. She had IDs for everyone on the hunt!"

From the bottom of the wallet, she pulled out three small ziplock plastic bags. Each contained thin plastic squares resembling microscope slides. "What the—?"

But Dan was intent on the leather notebook. "Check this out!" he said, examining a page full of scribbled phone numbers, calculations, and notes in Russian.

Amy repacked the wallet and stuffed it into her backpack. "I don't understand a word of this. . . ." She leafed through to the very last page and stopped.

Следующее место, 39 Ключи? От тетради RCH.

I'm with you and you're with me and so we are all together.

"We know what the 'thirty-nine' means," Dan said. "She was collecting information about the clues. Maybe this involves our next destination. Maybe she was going to give this to us — to help us!"

Amy's eyes watered. "She was on *our side*, Dan. How is that fair? Why hadn't she told us? Was she just pretending to be bad, or did she have a change of heart?"

Dan tried to smile. "Typical Lucian, huh? Sneaky and unpredictable."

"I can't believe you said that!" Amy snapped. "She saved our lives!"

"Hey," Dan said, "I was just kidding—"

"Lucians are liars," Amy went on in a mocking, singsong voice. "Tomas eat broken glass for breakfast, Ekaterinas are smart enough to build computers out of toe jam, Janus can write novels in their sleep, blah blah blah. Do you really think all of that is true, Dan? Then what about you and me? We're not like any of those. But we are in *one* of the branches."

Amy was in a mood. She needed a dose of lighten-up. Dan picked up Saladin and turned his face toward her, imitating a cat voice. "And what branch am I, the brave Saladin?" Dan purred. "E-CAT-erina? To-MOUSE?"

Amy turned away and began pacing, as if she hadn't even heard him.

The boat rode a steep swell again, and Dan felt his insides dance. He let out an involuntary *glurp*.

"*Whoaaaaa—AARRRGGGGGGGHHHH . . . shove two fingers down my throat and pull out my heart . . . to prove you love meeeee . . . !*" Clutching her iPod, Nellie emerged from the hatch and lurched toward them, like a creature put together from spare parts—a motion that Dan and Amy recognized as dancing. Pulling out her earbuds, she raised her face to the sky and let the rain pelt her for a few seconds. "Woo-hoo, that is better than a facial!" she cried, running to join Dan and Amy under the overhang.

"Stick around," Dan said, "for a lava treatment."

Nellie shook her hair dry and leaned against the wall. "Are you guys okay? Down below, I had a long talk with your uncle. He filled me in on all the details. What happened last night . . . what you saw . . . that was a lot to handle for a kid."

Dan nodded. "For anybody."

Amy wandered by, barely acknowledging Nellie. *"I'm with you and you're with me and so we are all together . . ."* she murmured under her breath.

Nellie burst out laughing. *"What* did you just say?"

"Some weird note," Dan began. "It was in—"

"Nothing!" Amy interrupted, whirling around. She was staring at Dan, the look in her eyes unmistakable: *We can't tell her. We can't trust her anymore.*

Dan glanced back helplessly. *If we don't trust Nellie,* he said with his eyes, *how will we get around? Who'll drive us—and pay for food and flights, and cover for the fact that we are two underage people traveling the world by ourselves? We have to tell her!*

Dan took a deep breath and looked away from his sister's piercing glance. "Okay. We saw that you had a bunch of coded e-mail messages."

"Dan!" Amy blurted.

"They were from someone named clashgrrl," Dan barged on. "The subject line said 'Status report' or something. And we also saw a text message. 'Keep them close.' Plus, we think it's weird that someone who can fly a plane has to work as an au pair."

"Whoa. You *spied* on me?" Nellie said.

"It wasn't like that—" Amy began.

Thunder echoed again. The boat tilted. Dan, Amy, and Nellie grabbed on to the metal poles that supported the overhang.

"You little sneaks!" Nellie practically had to shout to be heard over the rain. She shook her head and shrugged. "Well, at least you're honest. Okay, you really want to know? Clashgrrl? That's my homey from high school. We, like, talk about *everything*? Like, stuff that shouldn't be read by *nosy little kids*? Plus, she's an IT manager—total geek. She knows how to code messages and she does it with everyone. And FYI, she thinks I'm in the States, and 'keep them close' means two CDs of photos she gave me, to keep from her boyfriend, for reasons I don't want to tell you, thank you very much. And why I'm not, like, a *real* pilot yet is because my dad has this crazy idea I should be twenty-five before I even think of flying commercially. And that's why you got so lucky to have me. Any other questions?"

Dan felt like a total idiot. Amy was shuffling her feet, looking at the deck. "Sorry," Dan squeaked.

"Trust issues," Amy said.

"Apology accepted," Nellie said, glancing at Dan expectantly. "Your turn."

"Okay," Dan said, "the thing Amy said— 'I'm with you and you're with me' — it was a message Irina left. Probably a code, I'm thinking."

Nellie laughed. "Shut *up*! Irina said *that*?" She began flipping through her iPod playlists.

"You know it?" Amy asked incredulously.

"Voilà!" Nellie said, holding out the iPod screen.

Dan squinted at the album. "Velvet Cesspool . . . ?"

"The best. Band. Ever!" Nellie contorted her face into a pained expression and began to sing:

"I'm with you and you're with me!
And so we are all together!
So we are all together! So we are all together!
We are marching to Peoria! Peoria! Peoria!
We are marching to Peoria!
Peoria, hoo-RARRRRRAAAGGGHHHHHHHHH!"

"Huh?" Dan scratched his head. "I'm thinking Irina was more into, like, gloomy Russian church music."

Nellie held out the iPod toward Amy. "It's the album *Amputation for Beginners*," she said. "Third song, 'The Tracks of My Spit.' Go ahead, listen."

Amy inserted the earbuds. For a moment, her face got all lemony and puckered, which Dan found fun to watch. But soon she grinned and said, "Dan, don't you see? Our next destination is in the lyric! *That's* what Irina was trying to tell us, but she didn't have the chance to finish. It's right there at the end of the verse — the place they're marching to in the song!"

Dan pumped his fist in the air. "Woo-HOO! Bye-bye, Jakarta, hello . . ." His voice trailed off, his expression suddenly slack. "Peoria? As in, *Illinois*?"

"Well, no one said all Cahill ancestors had to live in exotic places," Amy said. "I'll bet Peoria is nice."

Behind them the hatch smacked open, and Uncle

Alistair staggered up into the rain. He was hunched and sleepy, and he carried an umbrella along with his cane. "My goodness, what a storm," he said, rushing to the overhang. "I confess I slept through most of it, until I heard this dreadful screaming—"

"That was *singing*, Al," Nellie shot back.

"Yes, well, I'm not exactly hep to the new styles," Alistair continued. "But, erm, those lyrics—There is a song I remember from the Harvard Glee Club. The song was brought to us, interestingly, by a bright young grad student from—"

Another bolt of lightning washed the eerily darkened sky in bluish white. As if on cue, the sea began to rise to the starboard side. Inside the cabin, Arif was shouting, his voice muffled by the sound of pelting rain.

"What's he saying?" Dan shouted.

Alistair was staring out into the fog. "Perhaps it is Indonesian for *we have company*!"

A red light was pulsing toward them.

"The police . . ." Dan said.

"Why would they suspect this boat?" Amy asked. "They're looking for the launch Nellie took!"

The boat's motor, which had been roaring against the force of the storm, now began to power down. Arif was heading out the cabin door, his arms in the air.

"He's giving us up!" Dan shouted.

"Of course," Alistair said. "If they catch us, he's an accomplice to a getaway. If he gives us up, he's a hero."

Nellie ran through the cabin door. "*Get belowdecks,*

right away!" she shouted over her shoulder. *"Go!"*

Before they could react, Nellie was sitting at the controls. The motor revved.

The bow rose up and the boat veered to the right. Alistair grabbed a pile of life vests. "Put these on!" he shouted, throwing vests to Dan, Amy, and Nellie.

Dan quickly donned his vest and scooped Saladin into his arms. He tried to get to the hatch, but Nellie was swinging the boat too sharply. He, Amy, and Alistair stumbled toward the stern.

Nellie had managed to slam the cabin door shut. Arif was banging on it, shouting.

"Hard to port, Nellie—that's the wrong side!" Alistair shouted through the cabin window. *"It will be too shallow!"*

The side of the boat now rose to starboard, and Dan's knees buckled. He slid across the deck, holding tight to Saladin. Alistair, trying to stand, lost his balance. Windmilling his arms, he staggered toward the side of the boat. Amy grabbed his arm, but the combined weight just gave him more momentum.

The deck angled higher. Dan reached out to brace himself against the gunwale, which was slanting ever closer to the water.

Alistair and Amy slammed into his side. He let go of Saladin.

The cat's scream was the last thing Dan heard before he and Saladin plunged into the Java Sea.

CHAPTER 4

"Saladin!" Dan screamed as his head popped above the water's surface.

Saladin was paddling, his wet fur matted to his face. He was all eyes, as if they'd grown twice their normal size. He seemed frightened to death.

"Dan . . . swim to shore!" cried Amy. She was to his right, treading water. "I see it. We're not that far!"

"Saladin!" Dan repeated.

"For heaven's sake, let the cat go!" Alistair cried out. "It's only an animal!"

Lightning flashed nearby, and Dan could hear a tree branch crack.

Dan could see two shapes converging toward him, large and small. One was the boat, tacking left and right as Nellie strained to see him over the steering wheel. The other was Alistair, swimming with slow, even strokes, somehow managing to keep hold of his cane.

Dan swam faster. He did not want to be grabbed in the water by anyone. Not before reaching Saladin.

"Gotcha!" As he grabbed the Mau and drew him close, Saladin yelped and scratched. "Easy, now . . ."

A wave slapped his face. He let himself rise with it, trying not to swallow. Trying not to let go of Saladin.

Where was the shore?

On the downwash of the wave, Dan looked desperately around for some sense of direction. Through the rain he could see a small flashing light. He began swimming, holding tight to Saladin. Alistair was soon by Dan's side. "Good, Daniel!" he cried.

"Mrrrrrooooowwwwwrr!" Saladin whined.

Amy was just ahead of him. The boat had stalled. Nellie and Arif were now by the railing, arguing in two different languages. Nellie was strapping on a life jacket and preparing to jump.

A wave broke over Dan's head and he gulped seawater. He could feel it filling up his lungs. Swimming with one hand was exhausting, even with a life jacket. The spray from the sea's surface blinded him. . . .

And then his head bashed into Amy's knee.

"REEOOOW!" screeched Saladin.

Dan's feet dropped — and he felt sand beneath him.

Saladin shivered, his chest pounding fast and hard. Dan stood, cradling the Mau in his arms. He glanced behind him for the police boat but could see nothing through the fog and rain. Swimming against the rough surf, Nellie shouted, "I'm at your back!"

"Are you okay?" Amy asked Dan.

Dan nodded. "I'm good. Thanks. Saladin, too."

As he watched Nellie stand in the shallows, a white light from the shore momentarily blinded him. Dan shielded Saladin's eyes as the light traveled to Amy, then Nellie. Finally, it settled on Alistair.

A hand came out of the mist, grabbing Dan and pulling him onto the sand. A couple of others reached out for Nellie and Amy.

"*Itu dia!*" a voice called out.

Alistair's voice, muffled but agitated, came through the pattering of the rain. "I beg your pardon, officers, unhand me! This is a mistake!"

"*Ikuti kami!*" the voice snapped back.

Dan turned to see one of the cops slapping a pair of handcuffs on Alistair and dragging him toward a van. Dan shook loose and ran toward them.

"Stay back, Dan!" Alistair shouted over his shoulder. "Isabel must have pinned the fire on *me*! I may be able to turn this to our advantage—but only if you don't make trouble! I can handle this."

"But—but they can't do this!" Dan shouted back.

One of the cops turned toward Dan.

Glorp. Dan swallowed his next words of protest. He sheltered Saladin in his chest and shrank back.

"Dan, stand still," Nellie commanded. "Both of you, be safe!"

Out of the corner of his eye, Dan could see the boat floating just offshore. Arif was still aboard, talking quietly into his cell phone.

The cop glowered at each of them and began pointing. *"Tetap di situ!* You, you, you, you . . . stay!"

Then, barking a command, he shoved Alistair into the van and shut the door. He slid into the driver's seat, and the van slipped away into the fog.

"It's a trumped-up charge," Nellie said. "It can't stick. He'll be out in no time."

"Why would Isabel pin it on him?" Amy asked.

Dan nodded, shifting the pet carrier from his right hand to his left. "*We* were the ones she wanted to kill. It doesn't make sense."

"I guess he took the hit for you," Nellie said. "You owe him, big-time."

Amy's shoes squished loudly as they all trudged into town from the dock. The rain had stopped as suddenly as it had started, and the late morning had a crisp feeling. After Alistair had been carted away, they'd retrieved their stuff from the boat, but everything was drenched—except for Dan's computer, which he had wrapped in plastic, in true Dan style. Alistair had been on Amy's mind a lot, but she didn't want to admit what she was thinking—that it wouldn't bother her a bit if he were jailed in Indonesia for a long, long time.

Owe him? For all Amy knew, Alistair could have staged the whole thing. To slip away again.

We gave him the clue. We trusted him.

How did he do it? And how did they end up trusting a guy . . .

A guy who was at our house the night of the fire and didn't do a thing to stop it.

"We don't owe him anything," Amy growled.

Dan looked at her, startled. "Hey, Alistair was ready to die for us last night."

"I think he's up to something," Amy said, "and Isabel may still be after us." The sun hit her eyes. It was peeking through trees now, dappling the water-darkened sidewalks, as if they'd already been through nighttime and fast-forwarded to another day. Just ahead, she could see taxicabs whizzing across a busy street. "Let's book a flight and get out of here."

Nellie exhaled. "Sure, no problem. My Visa's gone, but I can rack up my MasterCard. Remind me to enter the Peoria Lotto when we get there."

"Peoria . . ." Dan murmured. "No dissing the place but is anyone worried that we're *wrong* about this?"

"Hey, we decoded the message," Nellie said. "Plus, there are two Cahill Cluesters who know the song. Irina wrote down the words, and Alistair sang it in the Harvard Glee Club. It's a lock, dude."

"*Glee* Club . . ." Dan repeated. "What do they do, sit around and tickle each other?"

"It's an old-school word for chorus." Amy smiled. "Both Dad and Mom sang in their college glee clubs. When we were growing up, their friends would come over and do a cappella music. You know, songs without instruments? One guy would bring this sheet music. Grace would sometimes come to hear. I used to love listening. Especially some of these amazing songs in German and French."

"Figures you'd like the boring stuff," Dan said.

In her memory, Amy could see the men and women standing in the old living room, their reading glasses at half-mast on their noses. She could picture the ornate script of the song titles on the sheet music. . . .

And in that moment, she knew exactly what she needed to do next.

Just up the street was a stout tan-brick building with flags flying from either side of the front door. The words *Perpustakaan Umum* were carved into a marble stone above the entrance, and even though they were completely unfamiliar, she had a feeling she knew exactly what the building was. "Can we make a short stop here?"

Dan's skin was beginning to lose its color. "Oh, har-har. A library, right? Just to make me crazy. 'Cause there's no reason we would go into a library. Right? I mean, we don't need to research Peoria, do we?"

Amy began heading for the building. "Not Peoria. Something else."

"Not funny, Amy!" Dan called as she pushed open the heavy brass doors. "Amy . . . *Amy?*"

CHAPTER 5

Alistair Oh had nothing against brass wristwear, but handcuffs created unsightly marks on one's skin.

As the police van jounced along a road west of Jakarta, he carefully adjusted the metal shackle so it was *over* the cuff of his Egyptian-cotton shirt. This sort of thing was a good distraction from the chaos in his brain. Nothing made sense anymore—how could *Irina Spasky* be dead? Why had she saved him and the children?

He had only been able to stare in disbelief. He had been a coward, just as he'd been seven years ago . . .

Don't think of that now.

He had to keep his head clear. There were more immediate problems.

The car bounced over a pothole, and Alistair heard a grunt of complaint from the front. From the person who had framed him. The person he had stupidly assumed would be Isabel Kabra.

From the front passenger seat, a familiar gaunt old man turned stiffly. "Are you experiencing discomfort,

Alistair? You are certainly looking well for someone who died in Pukhansan Park."

Bae Oh's words cut through Alistair like a rusty blade. He stared at his uncle, trying to detect a shred of feeling in the steel-gray eyes.

As a child, Alistair had been afraid of Bae, from the day the old man took custody of him. Which was immediately after the mysterious murder of Gordon Oh, Alistair's father.

Bae had been second in line to the leadership of the Ekaterina branch. All that lay in his way was his brother Gordon. At Gordon's funeral, Bae appeared to be sobbing. Alistair was only five, but he never forgot staring at his uncle's cheeks and seeing they were bone dry.

The innocent wept. The guilty pretended.

"I commend you, Uncle, on your acting abilities," Alistair said. "They have improved since I was a boy. Did you convince the police that I set the fire?"

"I fail to understand your hostility toward me, Alistair," Bae said. "I do have a heart, you know. Your obituaries in the Seoul newspapers moved me, and I rejoiced when I learned you were alive. Even after that bit of drama in my office, which I must add was rather baffling. Has it occurred to you that you are being unfair to me?"

"An interesting claim, with me here in the back of a police car," Alistair said.

"First things first," Bae said. "Perhaps you would like to tell me how you survived the cave-in."

"Life must retain some of its mysteries, don't you think?" Alistair said. "You certainly have your own."

Bae sighed. "I tried my whole life to groom you, Alistair. You had so much potential. I thought we could share the duties of Ekat leadership—I as branch head, you as my successor. Why did you never take responsibility? Spending time with those wretched American children. Did I teach you nothing, my son?"

"I am not your son," Alistair said through tightly clenched teeth. "I am the son of Gordon Oh."

Bae bowed his head. "Dear, dear Gordon . . ."

Tell him, Alistair thought. *Confront him now.*

Why was it so hard to face up to Bae? Alistair had had the opportunity after the cave-in. He'd sneaked into Bae's office, scared away his secretary.

I had him all alone, but I walked away. I didn't do a thing. He. Must. Not. Scare. Me. Any. Longer.

Alistair took a deep breath. "I found the letter," he said calmly. "You wrote it on Oh stationery in 1948. A letter concerning a payment for the murder of Father."

Bae's eyes widened. "It was a payment for *driving*!"

"Five thousand dollars to drive across town—the exact day Father was murdered?" Alistair said. "With the command to 'destroy letter immediately'?"

"It was a lump payment to the limo company for several months' business. And for your information, we routinely destroyed *all* our correspondence!" Bae stared at his nephew in shock, slowly shaking his head. "Honestly, Alistair, you surprise me."

Alistair, you surprise me . . .

Alistair, you disappoint me . . .

Alistair, how could you have been expelled from college . . . AGAIN?

Alistair shook off memories that never seemed to fade, no matter how old he was. He was letting Bae into his soul again. *He will lie to your face because he knows you will lose your cool,* Alistair told himself. *And then, once again, he will own you.*

Alistair met his uncle's glance. "How am I to trust someone who lies to the police about his own nephew?" he said. "You know I didn't set the fire, and you will never make that charge stick."

Opening his overcoat, Bae patted a thick leather wallet that jutted from an inner pocket. "I have ways of influencing what sticks and what does not. And I can be persuaded to use that influence to your benefit."

Alistair laughed. "Lies and bribes, as always—"

"Unlike you, Alistair, I value the truth," Bae said. "You are an Ekaterina. And yet you withhold the truth from me, your erstwhile guardian and branch leader. All you need do is give what you owe me—the truth about what happened on that island, and all you have learned about Robert Cahill Henderson's discoveries."

"I . . . will . . . *never* . . ."

"Watch that blood pressure, my son," Bae said. "Your years as a failed junk-food magnate have taken their toll. Too many cheese burritos weaken the heart."

Alistair closed his eyes briefly and remembered

something his father told him, a phrase he had never understood as a child: *Silence is strength.* He breathed deep and then stared calmly at Bae Oh.

"Well?" Bae asked.

Alistair suddenly lurched back in the seat. His body convulsed once, twice. He gasped for air, flailing wildly, yanking the handcuffed arm of the cop.

The car was swerving now, toward the side of the road. The tires screeched. As the backseat cop tried to hold Alistair still, the driver swerved around.

"Keep going!" Bae shouted. "We have no time!"

"ARGGHH . . . GLLLLURGHHH!" Alistair sputtered. With a violent jolt of his upper body, he felt his head hit the roof and then collapsed, lifeless, on the backseat.

CHAPTER 6

Mildew. Rotting paper. Amy smiled. There was nothing more intoxicating than the aroma of old books.

In a small air-conditioned library room in Java, she set down a stack of music books from the library archives. The books were heavy, and they made a comforting thump on her table. Amy's backpack sat in a small puddle on the floor, and a young librarian rushed over with a towel to protect the cloth seats from Amy's wet clothes. She frowned, scolding Amy softly in Indonesian.

"Thanks," Amy said. "S-s-sorry."

Sheepishly she concentrated on the books, opening the top one first: *Glees, Shanties, Fight Songs, Madrigals, and Motets.* Just inside the cover was a stamp—the book had been donated by a local Harvard graduate.

As she opened the book, she heard a commotion by the door. The librarian and Nellie were chasing Saladin around the room. Dan skulked behind them. He shrugged at Amy. "Sorrrrry . . . I took him out for dinner and a cleaning. Now he's frisky."

"Got 'im!" Nellie said, snatching Saladin by the collar.

As Nellie scooted outside, Amy turned to her brother. "How is Saladin feeling?"

"Angry," Dan said. "After the bath, we found an Internet café. I checked a Mau-lovers' listserv? Oops, no red snapper in this area. He had to eat tuna."

But Amy didn't hear a word. She was too busy staring at a song title on page 47.

Fewer than a hundred miles away, on a highway outside the airport, Bae Oh watched his nephew in the throes of heart failure.

"Eccckkkk . . . Unc . . . Uncle . . ." Alistair cried out.

The driver was kneeling over Alistair, urgently talking on a cell phone while trying to hold his nephew still. The officer who had been cuffed to Alistair was fumbling with the keys to the cuffs.

"Good grief, men, *do* something!" Bae shouted.

Alistair reached up with trembling hands. He was gagging, his body contorted. Seeing him this way shocked Bae. Alistair had always carried himself with dignity. He had survived deadly explosions and massive collapses with nary a hair out of place.

How ironic that his own heart would do him in.

And nothing to show for it, Bae thought, *but a life frittered away.* College, business, and now health—Alistair had failed in everything. If only he hadn't been so soft. So ignorant of the uses of power. So willing to put others first. *College is needlessly competitive, Uncle . . . I want my own business to feed people at reasonable prices, Uncle . . .* By now he could have been *something* in the Ekaterina branch. Instead of a constant problem.

Ah, well, Bae thought, watching the life ebb from Alistair. *Often problems have unexpected solutions.*

The officer finally unlocked the cuff. As it fell away, Alistair's arm thudded heavily to the roadbed. His head lolled to the side. The officers were dumbfounded.

"Mati?" one of them muttered.

Dead, Bae translated silently.

He steadied himself on the police van. Alistair's eyes were open, staring. Accusing. In repose, he looked like his father. "Gordon . . ." Bae whispered.

Stop. It's not Gordon. It's the boy.

Struggling to stand, Bae walked farther into the road's shoulder, away from the noise of traffic. Leaning on his cane, he spoke into his cell. "Hello . . . I am calling to report the natural death of Alistair Oh. . . ."

"AAAAAAAGHHHH!" At the sound of an officer's scream, Bae hurried back toward the car.

He stopped short, dropping his phone and his cane.

The two officers were flat on the ground, writhing in pain. Alistair Oh stood between them, brushing himself off. He turned to Bae, nodded cheerfully, then scooped Bae's cane off the ground. "You dropped this, Uncle?"

Bae reached out. "But . . . but you were . . ."

"I may have been expelled from Harvard, but I

got an A in acting," Alistair said, flipping open the top of Bae's cane to reveal a collection of small black switches. "My, what have we here?"

Bae lurched forward. *"No, Alistair, you don't know what you're doing!"*

"Watch me," Alistair said. He swung the hilt of the cane toward Bae, releasing a black cloud of pepper spray.

Bae dropped to the road in a fit of coughing. His leg twisted. He heard a snap below the knee. Pain shot upward from his leg and downward through his lungs, and he felt as if his body were exploding.

He screamed, fighting to keep consciousness.

Alistair approached, the cane raised. "You look distressed, my dear, compassionate uncle."

Breathe. Eyes open. Focus. Bae stared at his nephew. Alistair had the perfect chance. One rap to the head was all it would take.

"AAGHH!" Alistair raised the cane over his head.

Bae closed his eyes. He heard a thump on the ground. He felt his hand being pulled upward. His back sliding against the grass. A cuff clanking shut on his wrist. Another on the car door handle.

Over the sound of his own shrieking, he was vaguely aware of a distant police siren piercing the air. And his nephew's voice, growing fainter and fainter.

Alistair was singing.

"I'm with you and you're with me and so we are all together. . . ."

CHAPTER 7

The Peoria International Airport had its share of mums and bored children. But rarely ones with an arsenal of poisons tucked into carry-on shampoo bottles, which made Ian Kabra quite proud.

The fact that the Cahill children had missed their flight did spoil things a bit. Not to mention the airport uniforms they were wearing.

"I can't believe we have to make ourselves look so . . . so . . ." stammered Natalie Kabra.

"Working class?" said Ian, whose airline security shirt was already making him itch. "Remember what Mother said. It's no longer so easy to infiltrate airline personnel. Be grateful for our Lucian contacts."

"Don't get me started on the little airplane name badges," Natalie grumbled.

"Will you two be quiet?" said Isabel Kabra as they rounded a corner, heading for the airport employee lounge. A brimmed SUPERVISOR cap could not hide the anger in her eyes as she hissed softly into her mobile: "Arif, speak *slowly*. My Indonesian is exceptional but not perfect . . . yes, I know you outwitted them . . . of course they didn't suspect you knew English, that is precisely why we pay you the big bucks . . . yes, I *saw* their names on the passenger list to Peoria, but *they were not in their seats*, Arif! . . . Ah, you have information on the next flight . . . *three hours?* Good. We shall hope they are on it. And, Arif . . . you should hope so, too." She flipped the phone shut, her face flushed.

"Well, then, happy news! *Hakuna matata* and all that," Ian said cheerily. "We'll rest and have a fine dining moment while we wait." He looked around at the various airport fast-food choices. "Well, er, we'll *rest* . . ."

"Three hours — here?" Natalie pulled on her starched collar. "Yesterday it was Tokyo, Paris, Vienna, Seoul, Sydney, and Java. I had *such* respect for the Cahills' location scouting. But — oh, honestly, Mother, that bumpy little puddle jumper to . . . P-Peo —" Her face turned green. "Excuse me, I'm not feeling well."

Ian watched her run off. "She has a point."

"Complaining about a location?" Isabel spun on her son. "When those children evaded us in Indonesia — twice? What does that tell you, Ian?"

"That they're lucky?" Ian guessed.

"Those children," his mother said, "are our only worthy adversaries."

Ian barked a laugh. "Good one, Mother!"

"Are you laughing at me, Ian?"

"No." Ian dropped the smile. "Then is it possible, Mother, that they have flown somewhere else?"

"Remember who is leading them," Isabel replied. "That nose-ringed nanny grafted to an iPod. It's a wonder they *ever* make a flight on time. No, Ian, we will not panic. They will be on the next flight they can manage to book. Remember, by our little arrangement with Bae Oh, we have taken out Alistair. Here in Peoria, they will be alone. To eliminate them, there must be no variables — *that* is the lesson of Indonesia."

Ian nodded. *Do not question her*, he told himself. *Not when she is in a state like this.*

Still, it was a pity to attack them with such force. Especially the girl, Amy. He'd never met anyone like her. Shy. Gentle. With an exciting edge of hostility. So unlike the girls back home, who flung themselves at him so often that his chauffeurs traveled with first-aid kits.

Doesn't she know better? Isn't she smart enough to stop the hunt?

It was the boy and the au pair. He was a pint-sized hothead. She was a collection of piercings and piggishness. If only Amy and Dan had stayed trapped in the cave in Seoul, at least long enough to get discouraged. Why did they antagonize Mother?

They don't know what it's like to live with her.

"Right you are," Ian said. "They're asking for it. Heaven forbid they listen to the brains of the outfit."

"And that would be — ?" Isabel said

Ian looked away. "Well, the sister, I'd say. Amy."

He felt a smile inching across his face.

"Ian?" His mother grabbed his wrist. "If you are

having the inkling of a shadow of a thought . . ."

"Mother!" Ian could feel the blood rushing to his face. "How could you suspect for a moment . . . ?"

"Mother! Ian!" Natalie was racing out of the bathroom now. She looked even sicker than before. "I just got a text message from Reagan Holt!"

Isabel Kabra looked aghast. "You texted a Tomas?"

"No! She hacked into my mobile." Dismayed, Natalie looked at the screen in her hand and began reading. "'Thanks, Nat. We managed to pick up Dan and Amy's next loction from your phine' -- oh, good grief, the spelling! — '*location* from your *phone*. We are on their tail, and if we smell a Lucian, WATCH OUT. ttfn, Reagan.'"

Ian groaned. The Holts were one of the more unpleasant aspects of this hunt — nasty, brutish, and dull. "So much for the Cahills being *alone*."

"Perhaps we can put a 'Tomas-Free Zone' sign on the landing strip," Natalie said. "That will confuse the dolts — sorry, *Holts* — for a day or so."

"Those dimwits," Isabel said with a calm smile, "may be good with a paraglider, but they will not stop us from isolating Dan and Amy here. And once we have them, we'll have some fun with this."

She pulled out a glowing green vial from her shoulder bag.

Ian swallowed hard.

"It's the liquid we snatched from the Cahills in Paris!" Natalie said. "Mother, you've made a mistake!"

Isabel glared at her daughter. "As *Ian* no doubt realizes,

this vial is a fake. Inside it is a poison. After we administer this, they will experience a slow deterioration of body function, culminating in a long hospital stay and then death." Isabel opened her shoulder bag to reveal a collection of hypodermic needles.

"I see," Ian said. "We, erm, force-feed them, as it were."

Natalie's face was turning green. "What if they . . . have an antidote?" she squeaked.

"A good question — by God, was that Natalie speaking?" Isabel said. "Well, yes, one of the family branches is rumored to have developed antidotes to Kabra poisons over the years. I always suspected Grace of being behind this. But oh, dear, I do suppose it's a bit too late for the children to run crying to her, isn't it?"

Ian flinched. He glanced toward his sister to see if she agreed, but she seemed intent on her mobile, as usual.

"Okay, change of topic?" Natalie said, looking up. "Um, do either of you know what red snapper is?"

"It's what some people eat when there is no lobster or caviar," Ian replied. "Why?"

"My RSS feed on Dan Cahill's name shows a request a few hours ago for . . . red snapper?" Natalie scratched her head. "For their cat!"

Isabel grabbed the phone so quickly her hat went askew. "Natalie — *where did that request come from?*"

"We are in Code Red."

The professor sat bolt upright. He had been only

half awake when he'd answered the mobile.

The call could mean only one thing. "They are here?"

"I am not at liberty to say," came a familiar gravelly voice. "But this is my final request of you."

With the phone tucked into his ear, the professor quickly, quietly dressed himself. "You know I cannot do as you wish. I am not one of your people."

"You have left the Tomas—"

"I am an educator," the professor said. "I believe in teaching. It is not necessary to cut each other's throats. This kind of thinking has hurt my country, my people—and the family."

He knelt over his laptop and keyed in the network password. Running the cursor down the left side, he clicked on the FLIGHT PASSENGER INFORMATION nav bar.

He scrolled through a list of flight rolls.

There. Just as he suspected.

Running out to the car, he kept his attention only half tuned to the voice at the other end. ". . . your goals are exactly the same as ours," it said.

"But our methods could not be more different." The professor spoke loud as he started the car, to blot out the engine noise. "I do not take joy in being feared. As I recall, neither did you, years ago!"

"Isabel Kabra has killed Spasky," said the voice. "She is getting angry. And sloppy. I have picked up an intercept on her phone. We must close ranks. We need you."

The professor barreled through a red light. A horn blared in his ear and he slammed on his brakes. As he swerved through the intersection, the sounds of motorists' curses rose up behind him like barking dogs. "How on earth — how did Irina die?" he shouted.

"While saving the children's lives!"

"What?"

"Where are you?" the other voice demanded.

The professor closed the phone. *Could it be?*

He pulled to the side of the road and let his breathing ease. Focus was necessary. For his own safety. For the safety of his fellow drivers. And, perhaps, for the peaceful end to a half millennium of needless violence.

Irina came to her senses. Irina is dead.

The chase was heating up. Loyalties were fraying.

He reached into the glove compartment and pulled out a small framed photograph. It was a portrait of a man dressed in full Zulu war gear, white feathers at his arms and calves. He wore a black-and-white headdress and held a full-body shield and a bladed weapon that was neither sword nor knife. His face was gaunt and severe, his skin nearly as coal-black as the Macassar oil that slickened his hair.

The professor placed the portrait on his seat. He drove on singing, as he always did to clear his mind. In twenty minutes he reached the airport. Flashing his badge to security, he entered the service road to the back of the terminal.

They would be arriving in a matter of minutes.

CHAPTER 8

Changing travel plans was one thing. Entering an airport in a strange country with a wet backpack that smelled like dead possum was a whole other story.

"Welcome to South Africa!" a flight attendant chirped.

"Thank you!" Hoping the aroma wasn't too noticeable, Amy raced out the door of the 767 and into the bustle of OR Tambo International Airport.

A day ago she wouldn't have dreamed they'd be here. But the library trip had set them straight.

"You'd better be right about this," Nellie muttered, grumpy after the uncomfortable night's sleep.

"Who farted?" Dan asked.

"It's our clothes," Amy said.

"Our clothes farted?" Dan asked.

"I don't know them, ladies and gentlemen," Nellie said under her breath, "never saw them in my life . . ."

Dan began sprinting off toward a sign that said CHECK YOUR E-MAIL/SURF THE WEB HERE! "Nellie, I'm going to use your MasterCard, okay?"

"Sure, just call me Cash Machine Gomez!" Nellie

took Amy's arm. "Tell me again why you decided to come here? I remember it was smart, and I remember making the decoy reservations to Peoria, but we did it when I was in a state of almost-asleepness."

Amy pulled from her pocket a copy of the sheet music she had found in the library: "Marching to Pretoria."

"It's a traditional song, performed by choruses all over the world," Amy continued. "Including the Harvard Glee Club. That's what Uncle Alistair was try-ing to tell us — the real lyric is *Pretoria.* In South Africa. It's much more likely Irina knew the lyrics to the origi-nal. She was telling us to go *here.*"

Nellie was keeping an eye on Dan, who was scroll-ing through a screen dense with text. "Don't rack up too many minutes, little dude. I'm not rich, especially when you make me buy decoy tickets. And I'm about to buy you phones."

"Arrrghhhh!" Dan cried out, bouncing away from the computer. "No, no, no, no, *no!*"

Amy nearly leaped into the air. She and Nellie bolted toward the web station.

"What, Dan?" Amy called out. "What happened?"

Dan sighed. "Just checked the listserv. No fresh red snapper in South Africa. Saladin's going to kill me."

<hr/>

If there was anything worse than waiting for a pet car-rier to appear, it was waiting for a pet carrier to appear while being lectured by a big sister about the history of South Africa. And Nellie was off buying cell phones and renting a car, so Dan was trapped.

"'. . . As gold and diamond deposits were found,'" Amy read from a pamphlet, "'more and more English miners flooded into the Transvaal region, which was controlled by the Dutch. Tensions over this eventually led to the Boer War.' Dan, that's when 'Marching to Pretoria' was written—it was all about the Boer War!"

"Hey," Dan said, "any country that sings about hairy pigs can't be all bad."

Amy groaned. "Not *that* kind of boar!"

"Oh . . . *Bore War!*" Dan said. "That's so you, Amy. What'd they do, read history to each other until one side went '*GAAHHH!*' and surrendered?"

"*B-o-e-r,*" Amy said. "It's the Dutch word for *farmer.* Most of the original seventeenth-century settlers were Dutch, German, and French Huguenot farmers and cattle herders. They also became known as Afrikaners."

Dan's eyes started to glaze, and he ran right into an older man dressed in a shabby jacket and ripped pants. "Sorry," he squeaked, bouncing quickly away.

The man was giving him a quizzical smile. His skin was dark brown, with a curved scar running along his jawline, and his gray-green eyes seemed to dance in the fluorescent light.

"Do you need a car service?" he asked. "Or can spirited young people like yourselves navigate South Africa on your own?" He handed Dan a postcard.

"Uh, no thanks," Dan said.

"Keep it anyway," the man said. "Just in case! You never know when you will need Slimgaard!"

As the man left, Amy walked over. "What was that about?" she asked, an eye still on the conveyor belt.

Dan glanced at the card:

SLIMGAARD

LIMOS

THE ART OF SERVICE, THE HOPE OF MANKIND.

WE ARE ALWAYS WITH YOU!

— Bimrsesoseim Gekk #4

— Bgoqbg Gekk

ALPHA > 1

POSKAART
POSTCARD

SLEGS VIR ADRES
FOR ADDRESS ONLY

"'The hope of mankind'?" Amy said. "A limo service with a handwritten card?"

Dan flipped it over. The other side had an image of a tall African man holding a shield, with what looked like an encyclopedia entry underneath:

Shaka, 1787–1828. Founder of Zulu Nation. Son of a Zulu tribal king and a woman, Nandi, from another kraal. His birth was considered shameful; his name means "intestinal parasite." Shaka and Nandi were exiled, only to be abused by other local tribes. At 16, Shaka turned his rage on an attacking leopard and killed it single-handedly. With brawn and cunning, he rose to power, fueled by vengeance. Shaka scorned tribal war tactics of the time, spear-throwing from long distances, and perfected close combat with short, large-bladed spears. His famed "buffalo horn" attack strategy helped build a military force that overtook local tribes and created one of the most powerful kingdoms ever known. Although many modern historians decry his violence, Shaka is considered the father of the united Zulu nation and a hero to South Africans.

"Cool," Dan murmured to himself, staring at the image of Shaka.

"Woo-hoo—look! Saladin's here!" Amy was now running over to the baggage claim conveyor belt. In a moment, she was walking back with the pet carrier. "Want to be the first to open it and say hi?"

But Dan couldn't take his eyes off the image of Shaka's shield. "Amy," he said, "what do you see here?"

"Um . . . Saladin's starving and you're looking at a cheesy tourist postcard?" she replied.

"His shield," Dan said. "Take a look at his shield."

Amy nearly dropped the pet carrier to the floor—and Dan instantly knew he wasn't seeing things.

In the center of Shaka's shield was the Tomas crest.

CHAPTER 9

Amy had come within an inch of being flattened by a subway train. She had escaped collapsing buildings and been trapped in airless tombs. But waiting for Dan outside a bookstore was a shock she never anticipated.

"Maybe we should find a doctor," Nellie murmured. She handed Amy a recycled cell phone she had bought at an airport shop.

"Thanks—well, at least he's interested in something," Amy said, pocketing the phone.

Dan was grinning as he left the airport bookshop with a biography of Shaka Zulu. "Thanks, guys, this is awesome. They didn't have anything by the Gekks, but this one looked cool."

"The Gekks?" Amy asked.

"The people who wrote the text on the Shaka card." Dan flashed his postcard. "I can't pronounce their first names, but I like their style. Hey, how's Saladin?"

Hearing his name, Saladin scratched the side of his pet carrier. It was amazing how much anger could be contained in a *mrrp*.

As Dan knelt in front of the pet carrier, Nellie grabbed his arm. "Who-o-o-oa! The last time you did this, I ended up chasing that cat all over a library. Best behavior, guys. The rental-car clerk is eyeing me. It was hard enough convincing her to rent to me. I'm scared she's going to change her mind. Oh, and here's your phone, Dan. Don't say I never gave you anything."

Nellie grabbed the carrier and headed down the corridor. Dan followed her, leafing through the Shaka biography. "Nothing Cahill-ish in the index. He's got to be descended from Thomas, right?"

Amy shook her head. "Thomas Cahill settled in Japan. Shaka's parents were members of African tribes—and none of them had seen Europeans. Ever. Shaka didn't meet any Europeans until, like, the 1800s. Right?"

"Right . . ." He leafed through his Shaka book. "Some guy from a British delegation—Fynn—saves Shaka's life. Heals a sword wound, gives him meds. Hair dye, too. When Shaka sees his gray hair disappear, he's, like, whoa, they made me younger. It's magic! Up till then, Shaka hasn't liked the Europeans. Now he realizes, hey, they have something I need."

"The hair dye?" Nellie said.

"The weapons," Dan answered. "So now he's, like, okay, I trust them. Which ends up being a bad call."

Nellie led them to an elevator. "The point is, if he wasn't descended from a Cahill, he couldn't be one," Amy said. "So how did he get a shield with a Tomas crest?"

"A certified pre-owned shield store?" Dan replied. "I don't know. Let's do some more research on him."

"I can't believe *you* suggested that."

"Shaka's fun, not boring," Dan said. "The Zulus did this killing head-twist? *Snnnap*—dead. They impaled enemies on stakes, then planted them like trees! Shaka was a genius. He's, like, what's up with spear-throwing, dudes? It's like throwing fly balls. The bad guys just step out of the way—plus, you lose the spear! So he teaches everyone to shish-kebob enemies with recyclable swords—green combat! His archrival, a dude named Zwide? Shaka fed his mother to the jackals. Who *wouldn't* want to research someone like that?"

"Sounds like a real laugh riot," Amy said flatly.

The elevator door opened, and Nellie stepped into the car-rental lot. "The chariot waits, kids. We're looking for slot thirty-seven K."

Dan followed her into the lot and scanned the area. *"Whoa . . . you ordered a Hummer? WOO-HOO!"*

Yipping with glee, he sprinted toward an enormous black Hummer near a post labeled 37K.

Nellie examined her receipt. "I said the cheapest car. Even one with holes in the floor, like the Flintstones."

Amy counted to seven before she heard what she expected—a devastated *"AAGHHHH!"* from Dan. They found him slumped against a yellow two-door Yugo, looking forlornly to his right, where the Hummer sat in the slot marked 38K. "I was off by one."

Nellie looked inside. "Sweet. A stick shift!"

"I think you should demand an upgrade," Dan said. "Look at this hunk of junk. The steering wheel in on the wrong side!"

"They're all like that," Nellie said. "They drive on the wrong side of the road here."

"The rental clerk insulted your honor!" Dan pressed. "Shaka Zulu would not have settled for a Yugo."

"Dude, this was hard enough to get," Nellie said.

Amy backed away from her brother and au pair, leaving them to their argument. She crept around to the other side of the Hummer. There was something strange about it. The windows were dark, a dusky black. But they were also fogged.

She leaned in to the driver's side, peering through the window. She couldn't see much, but the front seat seemed to be shaped funny—lumpy, not straight across.

Then the lump moved.

Dan reluctantly settled into the front seat of the Yugo, putting Saladin's carrier on his lap. The seats were hard. "Smells like fish in here," Dan said.

"At least Saladin will like it," Nellie replied.

"*Now* can I let him out?" Dan said, beginning to unlatch the pet carrier straps.

But Amy was flinging open the passenger door, diving into the backseat. "Go! *Go!*"

Next to them, the Hummer began to bounce. From inside came the sound of shouting voices.

"Someone's in there?" Dan said.

"They were waiting for us!" Amy shouted.

"I thought they were all in Illinois!" Nellie slammed on the gas and threw the stick shift into reverse. The car jumped off the ground and jolted backward.

EEEEEEEEEE . . .

"You're right, this *is* a piece of junk," Nellie said.

Dan felt Amy's arm reach over his shoulder and grab the pet carrier. "Give me this before Saladin goes flying out the window!"

With a screech of tires, the Yugo peeled backward out of slot 37K. Nellie yanked the steering wheel to the right and the car did a ninety-degree turn. "Yee-*hah!*" she screamed, throwing the car into first gear.

Dan was looking over their shoulders. "Um, Amy, they're not following us."

"That's because I took these." Amy held up a set of keys. "The front door was open and I reached in."

"Whoa, snnnap!" Dan said. His sister was all grinning and proud of herself. "You took your Cahill pills!"

THUNK. The car jounced over a traffic barrier and into the streets. Dan didn't know what to expect of Johannesburg, but he didn't see much of anything here, just dry fields stretching out in all directions.

"Guys? How do we get to Pretoria?" Nellie asked.

"Northeast," Amy said, leafing through a pamphlet. "Ought to be about a half hour. There's a major library, the State Library. Also the government archives, the University of South Africa, the National Cultural

History Museum. We ought to be able to find some connection between Shaka and the Cahills."

"Northeast . . ." Nellie said, peering out the window to her left. "Let's see. The sun is rising in the east . . ."

"Watch it!" Dan shouted.

The Hummer zoomed around them from the left, cutting sharply in front.

"How'd they get a set of keys so fast?" Nellie said.

"Now you did it," Dan shouted. "They're mad!"

"Hurry!" Amy said.

"I'm going as fast as I can!" Nellie yelled.

She wove in and out of traffic, whizzing past a sharp right-hand exit. "Nellie, get off this road!" Dan said.

"She can't," Amy replied. "She's past the exit—"

"Not yet!"

Nellie yanked the steering wheel right. The Yugo tilted sharply, its left wheels lifting off the ground as it veered onto the grassy shoulder.

The car bounced, its front bumper crunching down repeatedly on the rock-hard dirt. Its rear wheels began sliding side to side, kicking up dust clouds. Inches away, the road dropped off sharply into a steep ditch.

"Hang on!" Nellie cried out.

"We're going to die!" Amy shouted.

She closed her eyes as the car sailed into the air.

CHAPTER 10

Dan had no idea that dying felt so bad on the tongue.

"OWWWW . . . ow-ow-ow-ow-ow!" he screamed, blood trickling over his bottom lip.

His eyes opened. The Yugo was in the ditch, slanted to the right. Nellie gunned it forward, her left tires just gripping the ditch's upper ridge. "HANG ON!"

With a loud bump, the car lifted upward onto the lip of a downhill exit ramp. It swerved, straightened, and picked up speed.

Dan sucked back the blood from his bitten tongue, which was beginning to swell. He watched the dust settle around them. Nellie had managed to backtrack to the exit ramp she'd passed, and they were headed into a bleak-looking area just short of the city skyline.

How did she learn to drive like that?

"You did it!" Amy cried out. *"You got away!"*

"Why did oo haf thoo do that?" Dan said, his tongue thick and throbbing. "I bit my thongue!"

Nellie was staring angrily forward, leaning on her horn. "Hey, *who taught you idiots how to drive?*"

There was a car headed directly toward them.

"The *left* side of the road, Nellie!" Amy shouted. "They drive on the left!"

"Oh, right. Brain fart."

Nellie adjusted into the left lane and gunned it. She zoomed through an intersection, not stopping for any of the cars. Hugging the left side of the road, Nellie sped past whitewashed buildings and chicken-wire fences, past women balancing buckets on their heads and men three-to-a-seat on motorcycles.

A screech of tires made Dan spin around. Through the rear window he spotted the Hummer stuck in the intersection, surrounded by honking motorists.

Nellie pushed the Yugo to its limits. The town was small, and the four-lane road soon narrowed to two. Outside the town, the countryside was flat and green, with distant outcroppings resembling enormous stone fists. Cattle grazed in pastures, and the land was dotted with tin shacks and wood huts.

"We really lost them," Amy said.

But Dan had his eye on the back window. A faint hum grew louder, like an approaching plane.

And then, through the dust, a wide black silhouette purred its way up the street.

Dan's tongue felt like a wad of paper towel. "Hummuh!" he said. *"HUMMUH!"*

As Nellie sped over a hill, a flock of goats ambled across the road. The goatherd was a craggy old man singing to himself and beating the ground rhythmically with a staff. Seeing the car, the goats lifted their heads as if to say, *Sorry, WE were here first.*

"YO, GET OUT OF THE WAY!" Nellie screamed.

"They're *goats*!" Amy said. "They don't understand English!"

"NO-O-O-O-O-O!" Dan shouted.

Nellie slammed on the brakes. The Yugo arced to the left, onto the parched plain. Dan listened for the sound of goat massacre but heard only the crunching of rock underneath them.

Then, from behind them, a hollow, unearthly *EEEEEEEEEEEEEEEEE* . . .

Dan opened his eyes. The Yugo was careening across open ground. Goatless.

The smell of burning rubber reached him from behind. He turned to look out the back window.

The goats were thick in the road now, still chewing, still bleating, still alive and safe. The Hummer had narrowly missed the flock and disappeared headfirst into a chicken coop. A cloud of white feathers plumed up around it, and some very angry birds were expressing their disapproval.

A farmer drove up to them in a purple-painted pickup and hopped out, yelling.

Dan sat back and let out a sigh of relief. He rubbed his tongue against his lips, trying to stop the pain, as Nellie aimed the car back onto the highway.

CHAPTER 11

When Dan's eyes opened from a nap, the Yugo was parked under a tree at the top of a hill. Below them was a field where a group of men played soccer.

He pressed his tongue against the top of his mouth. The tip was still sore, but the swelling had gone down. "Owwww . . ."

"Where are we?" Amy said groggily.

"Lunch stop," Nellie said. "Just outside Pretoria. There's a food shop up the road. I figure we'll hide the car here in case our friends come looking for us."

"Um, guys?" Dan said, looking past Amy. "Is that what I think it is?"

Amy whirled around. A hulking purple pickup truck trailing white feathers was lumbering up the road toward them.

"Why would that be here?" Amy said. "It belongs to the farmer whose chicken coop the Hummer destroyed."

"Unless the Hummer dudes hijacked it!" Dan said.

"Come on!" Nellie hopped in the Yugo and turned

the ignition key. The car sputtered and wheezed. She tried again and it died.

"Run!" Amy said.

They sprinted down toward the soccer field. The players stopped, staring at them in bafflement. Beyond the field, the hill swept upward into a dense thicket of trees. It would be easy to get lost there.

Amy climbed, keeping right behind Nellie. But when they reached the top, Dan wasn't with them.

"What the — ?" Nellie said.

Dan was talking to one of the soccer players, gesturing back toward the pickup. The man was nodding intently as other players gathered around them.

"Dan!" Amy started to call out, but Nellie put her hand over her mouth.

In a moment, Dan was scooting up the hill. "Move!" he said. "We need to hide!"

"What were you doing?" Amy hissed.

"Run now, chat later." Dan scampered past them into the woods, finding a path that followed along the ridge. When the soccer field came in sight again, he ducked behind a thick bush. "We'll wait," he said. "If everything goes right, there will be a huge fight down there. We'll circle back to the car and try again."

Amy and Nellie knelt on either side of him. On the field, the soccer team had closed around five people dressed in elaborate, colorful African robes and odd feathered hats. One guy, who appeared to be captain of the players, was gesturing heatedly.

In a moment, Amy and Dan's pursuers were shedding their robes. The burliest one was the first to remove his hat.

The bristling, brush-cut scalp of Eisenhower Holt was instantly recognizable. As was the slavering pit bull that was bounding around the sidelines.

"The *Holts*?" Dan said.

Amy grabbed Dan's arm. "Those were the clothes they were wearing when I saw them crouched down in the Hummer. It's their idea of a disguise. What did you tell the players?"

"The truth, sort of," Dan replied. "That the people in the truck were a gang of bad guys chasing after innocent kids. Now, come on, let's get ready to move."

Amy glanced to her left, following the path they would need to take to the car. For at least fifty yards, they would be totally exposed.

Below, Eisenhower was shouting at one of the players. Pushing him. But Hamilton was on the sidelines, combing his hair in a hand mirror. Preening.

The sun's reflection glinted from Ham's mirror. Dan recoiled, shielding his face with his hand. "The jerk."

The glare landed on Nellie. "Ow! Oh, thanks a lot. Let's get out of here."

"Wait," Amy said. "I think he's *aiming* it."

Dan became rigid. "Whoa. Hold still, Nellie. He's sending a message!"

"A *what*?" Nellie said.

"*Dit-dit-dit, dah-dah-dah, dit-dit-dit,*" Dan muttered.

"The standard Morse code distress signal. Hamilton is sending Morse code! This is, like, so World War Two!"

He took his Shaka card from his pocket and gave it to Amy. "Hold this up. Try to catch the mirror message as best you can. I'll write down the letters."

"You know Morse code?" Nellie said.

"Duh," Dan replied.

By the time Dan got out a pencil and candy wrapper, the flares had stopped. But they began again as Amy held up the card.

Dan whispered as he wrote: *"Dah-dah-dit . . . dah-dah-dah . . . dah-dit . . . dah-dah-dah . . . dit-dah-dah . . . dah-dit-dit-dit . . . dit . . . dit-dah-dah . . . dit-dah . . . dit-dah-dit . . . dit . . ."*

Hamilton abruptly put his mirror in his pocket and ran onto the field. The African players were teasing him in a mixture of English and some other language.

"What's it say?" Amy asked.

Dan showed what he'd written:

Dan read the letters. "'Gon ow be ware'?" he said.

"Um, I'm just a stupid au pair," Nellie said, "but wouldn't that be, *Go now. Beware?*"

RRRROMMMMMM . . . CHCK! CHCK-CHCK-CHCK.

Amy looked up at the sound.

At the top of the ridge, about twenty yards farther in and well out of sight of the clearing, the yellow Yugo had pulled to a ragged stop in a clearing. The driver's window was begrimed with dirt.

A shiny two-tone dress shoe emerged from the car first, planting itself on the ground, followed by a pair of cream-colored linen pants.

"Greetings, my beloved niece and nephew," said Alistair Oh.

CHAPTER 12

"You're . . . here!" said Amy. "How did you escape?"

"How did you find us?" Dan asked.

"How did you start the car?" said Nellie.

"All will be explained in the fullness of time, my dears." Alistair gestured urgently toward the door. "I suggest we enter the chariot and ride away from our well-muscled nemeses."

"I'll drive!" Nellie raced around to the driver's side.

"Let me," Alistair said, blocking her way.

Amy stepped forward, then stopped in her tracks.

Go now. Beware. That was the warning.

Hamilton doesn't mean "beware the Holts," she thought. *He means "beware Alistair."*

"No, Nellie!" Amy shouted. "Don't get in there."

Amy fixed Uncle Alistair in her vision. He was cocking his head to one side, his yellow silk scarf gently wrinkling with the motion.

"Where do you go when you leave us?" Amy asked.

"Amy . . . ?" Alistair said, wiping his forehead with a white handkerchief.

Amy took a deep breath and counted to three. It was a technique Mom had taught her. Sometimes that was all it took to check your heart against your brain. "Think about this, Dan. We open our hearts to him every time. He swoops in to save us. We give him whatever we find. Then he vanishes. What does he do with the information? And how did he and the Holts find us at the same time — in the middle of South Africa?"

Dan looked uncomfortably at Uncle Alistair. Nellie retreated from the car door.

"If you must know," Alistair said, looking nervously down the hill, "I was held in Indonesia under false pretenses, but I escaped. I gambled on the notion that you were marching to Pretoria, as it were, but most international flights come in to Johannesburg. I was able to convince some airline personnel to reveal flight lists to me. It took detective work among the rental-car people to find which car you took, but we Ekats are good at that. I hired a driver to head for Pretoria. That was when I saw the Hummer, which made me suspicious."

"And you followed it . . ." Amy said.

"Precisely," Alistair replied. "Now may we go?"

"Wait," Dan said. "How did the *Holts* find us?"

"*We can talk inside the car!*" Alistair said.

"You're a smart guy," Amy said. "You heard Nellie sing the song and *boom!* You knew the hint. You're light-years ahead of anyone. And you're telling us that the *Holts* figured all of this out without your help?"

Alistair cocked his head curiously. "Are you

suggesting I am in an alliance with the *Holts*? I can't even carry on a conversation with them!"

"Come on, troops," Nellie said, reaching for the car door. "Let's leave Old Burrito Man here with the Frankenstein family. Maybe when they find out their plan failed, they'll use him as a soccer ball."

Nellie was in the car now. She turned the engine over once . . . twice . . . three times, and it finally started.

"You're not going to leave me here, are you?" Alistair was looking at Amy now. His face registered shock, panic. It was an expression she recognized from the fire two nights before.

He was willing to save our lives. He was about to jump off a ledge for us, until Irina arrived.

But she also knew the look from another time. From seven years ago. When he had come to their house to steal a poem. A poem with a Clue hidden in it. A poem that Hope Cahill and Arthur Trent thought would solve the riddle of the 39 Clues.

We only want what is ours.

Someone had said that during the night. She'd heard the voice from the study, just after the commotion had wakened her.

Alistair's voice.

Alistair hadn't set the fire. But he could have said something. He could have prevented . . .

"Amy . . . ?" Alistair said. "Are you all right, dear?"

Amy looked him in the eye. "Why did you keep it from them — the fact that you'd stolen the poem?"

"I—this is hardly the time—" Alistair stammered.

"You could have told them," Amy said. "You could have shouted, 'I have the poem!' She was running into a fire, Uncle Alistair!"

"I was contending with so many people," Alistair said. "I could barely see straight. Eisenhower Holt had some cockamamie idea that we could use the neighbors' garden hose—"

"Eisenhower Holt was there, too?" Amy said.

"And his wife, Mary-Todd," Alistair said.

Dan's face was red. "How many people were there—just standing around, doing nothing to help them?"

Eisenhower.

Yes, Amy saw him now in her memory of the night. A gruff man with a red face and bristles for hair.

They were all in it together. United. They may not all have set the fire, but without them it wouldn't have happened.

They were killers, all of them.

Tears rushed to her eyes, but Amy kept them back. Without thinking, she grabbed Uncle Alistair's silk scarf and pulled him toward her. "I don't care if you're working with them or not," she said. "Either way, when they find you, they will make your life miserable."

She let go and jumped into the backseat next to Dan. Nellie gunned the engine.

"Wait—you can't—" Alistair sputtered, struggling with something at the top of his cane.

"Oh?" Nellie said, stepping on the gas. "Watch me."

Alistair Oh staggered away from the cloud of exhaust and dust. He had never seen the girl so angry.

Dealing with the children was going to be nearly impossible now.

You knew to expect this, old boy, he told himself. *They are Grace's grandchildren.*

They were smart. Too smart. They had read him almost perfectly. If only they hadn't misread his motives.

The Holts, as usual, had ruined everything. Goodness knows how those blockheads had picked up the trail in South Africa! Or how they had managed to ambush him at the airport. The ride in the Hummer and the chicken truck had been grueling, but it hadn't compared with the humiliation of being their decoy.

They're scared of us, Alistair, but not of you, Mary-Todd had said. *We'll advance slowly and scare them. You sweep behind and drive them to us.*

Or die, Eisenhower had added.

Alistair dusted himself off and lifted his cane. None of them remembered that Oh Enterprises had been a proud NASCAR sponsor. None of them knew how Alistair Oh could handle even the lowliest automobile.

He glanced down the hill. The argument still raged. Soon it would be over, and the Holts would be after him. He would have to flee on foot while he had a chance.

Turning toward the road, he noticed a glint of silver in the dust — a cell phone. Most likely dead, but perhaps the aftermath of some recent picnic. If it worked, he could use it to call a car service.

Picking it up, he noticed a text message notification. He pressed READ.

SBS! M347.

How sad that people no longer communicated in real words. By now he had mastered "omg," "osm," "imho," "lol," "ttfn," and "rofl" — but not "sbs." *Such Boffo Shenanigans* perhaps. *Sis Boom Shazam? Super Bowl Sunday.* He winced as he remembered *Sushi Burrito Special*, a notorious product line that led to his company's demise. He'd been so obsessed with the hunt for the 39 Clues that he'd neglected to oversee the proper storage, resulting in the illness of thirteen people. And bankruptcy.

He clicked through the various menus, trying to find some sort of ID. But it was fruitless. Finally, holding the phone to his ear, he tapped out the number for information.

Static. Broken sound.

He tossed the phone back onto the ground and carefully placed his fallen bowler back on his head.

Thwock.

A soccer ball knocked it off again.

"Freeze," came a rough voice from behind him. "Hands in the air and about-face — *harch*!"

Alistair tried not to shake as he turned.

"I hope," Eisenhower Holt said, "you play good defense."

CHAPTER 13

Dan wondered how Shaka Zulu would handle a ride in a busted Yugo with two females arguing over hotel accommodations.

"You're the one who worries about money," Amy said. "A tent is perfect. We'd use it every day."

"I need a mirror, clean sheets, and those little paper-wrapped soaps," Nellie said. "I collect them. If you use them at home they remind you of where you've been—"

"This search is *not* about comfort," Amy said. "You're being like the Kabras and Alistair—pampered and fussy. First it's the secrets, and now it's—"

"Excuse me, Little Miss Anger Management," Nellie interrupted. "What's happened to *you*?"

"OFF WITH YOUR HEADS!" Dan announced.

"Cram it, Shaka," Amy said dully.

But Dan ignored her. A brave warrior never took the bait. He was fighting to focus on the Shaka postcard, now wrinkled and sweat-soaked after their adventure. He stared at the last lines:

BIMRSESOSEIM GEKK #4
BGOQBG GEKK
ALPHA>1

"This doesn't look right," he said.

"Lots of African words have odd pronunciations," Amy began lecturing. "Like, you make a clicking sound while saying it, like the *Xhosa* tribe."

The way Amy said the word, it was like a tongue-click followed by *-osa*.

"Right, but those words have, like, Xs and exclamation points in the middle and stuff," Dan said. "These are different. They don't look African. They just look . . . weird."

"If it's not *African* weird, maybe it's *Dutch* weird," Nellie said. "They use lots of double letters. My aunt married a guy named Vanderdoonk."

Amy was peering at the names closely. "The brothers Gekk? I told you, those are the limo drivers. This is a business card for a taxi service."

"What about the stuff *under* the name?" Dan asked.

"'Alpha more than one,'" Amy said. "Alpha means 'A'—like, the best. They're bragging. Advertising."

Dan began to write. He scribbled the alphabet across the top of the card. "I'm thinking it's a code. 'Alpha' means 'alphabet.' 'More than one' is actually an arrow pointing to the right. It could mean 'substitute each letter with the one to the right'—like, B becomes C."

"You actually think like that?" Nellie asked.

Dan began replacing the letters one by one.

CJNSTFTPTFJN HFLL #4

"Like I said, it was a dumb idea," Dan said.

"Whoa, wait," Amy said. "What if instead of a simple substitution code you, like, replace each *consonant* with the next *consonant*, and each *vowel* with the next *vowel*? Like, B becomes C but I becomes O?"

"You, too?" Nellie said.

Dan began writing again:

CONSTITUTION HILL #4

"Bingo!" Amy exclaimed. She leafed through pamphlets she had stashed in the glove compartment. "Constitution Hill . . . it's a region in Johannesburg. The site of an old jail. Number Four must be an address."

"Johannesburg?" Nellie said. "I thought we were marching to Pretoria!"

"Don't forget the other Gekk name," Dan said.

Quickly, he decoded it, using Amy's method:

CHURCH HILL

"'Church Hill' — find that!" Dan said.

Amy shook her head. "Nope. No such place. We'll need to get a better map. But at least we have a start. Okay, Nellie, we have to go back in the direction of the airport, toward Johannesburg!"

"What if *Church Hill* is the thing that's in Pretoria?" Dan said. "I mean, we're here already!"

Nellie slammed on the brakes and glided into a

turnoff at the edge of the road. "Whoa, whoa, guys. I've been stunt-driving in a Yugo, running from Holts, dissing old men, and barely avoiding death by goat. I'm, like, ready to drop. I will take you wherever you want, but I want to finish what I started with Amy—and *I* get to pick where we stay, okay? I say, hotel. And I say, book it now or we sleep in the car." She reached into her pocket. "Do either one of you guys have my cell phone?"

"Nope," Amy and Dan said at the same time.

Nellie looked on the floor, then in the glove compartment. "Weird. I had it back on that field."

"The Holts are probably kicking it through the goal post," Dan said.

"Uh, dude," Nellie said. "This is no joke. I have to have that phone."

"The phone company has your stuff saved online," Dan said, "with all your boyfriends' numbers—"

"Not funny," Nellie said. *"You don't get it! I need that phone!"*

Dan gave Amy a look. This was not Normal Nellie.

"Now who's got a problem with anger management?" Amy said quietly.

Nellie took a deep breath and hung her head over the steering wheel. "Okay. Sorry. I'm losing my head. May I use your phone, Amy?"

Amy handed over her phone. As Nellie made her call, Dan pulled out his and quickly accessed his e-mail account. He stared at the most recent message:

```
we won. 10-7.
ilikeike
```

"Hey, Amy," Dan said, showing the screen to his sister. "Do we know anyone with this name?"

"Ilikeike . . ." Amy shrugged. "Looks Hawaiian."

Dan typed back:

```
um, gr8. who ru?
```

A moment later the response came:

```
meat 100 m n of BOOM on P Kruger
    or tacoman go BOOM
        ilikeike
```

"It's a wrong number," Dan said.

"Wait," Amy said. "It's not Hawaiian. *I like Ike* was a presidential campaign slogan from the 1950s!"

"Historical facts make me quiver with excitement," Dan said.

"For President Dwight David Eisenhower!" Amy said. *Eisenhower.*

Dan stared at the screen. "'Tacoman' . . . but Uncle Alistair was burritos . . . yup, that would be something Eisenhower would write."

"Exactly!" Amy said. "And I'm thinking *m-e-a-t* is supposed to be *m-e-e-t*. He wants us to meet him — or something bad is going to happen to Uncle Alistair."

"Guys, what if this is a trap?" Dan asked.

"What if it's not?" Amy replied. "Think about it, Dan.

The Holts found Alistair on that hilltop after we left. If he was working with them, they'd be mad at him, because he didn't deliver us. If he wasn't working with them, they'd be just as mad to find him interfering."

"We can't just ignore this," Nellie said.

"Yes, we can," Amy blurted. "Why do we have to run all over a strange country and risk our own lives? Why do we owe Alistair anything?"

Dan glanced at his sister uneasily. "Amy . . . ? I know you don't really mean that, right?"

His sister turned away, her face red. She took a breath and murmured something he took to mean yes.

"Okay . . ." Dan nodded. "'One hundred m n' . . . that's one hundred *meters north* of — what's Boom?" He grabbed Amy's map of Pretoria. On the right side was an alphabetical list of street names. "It's a street — Boom Street on the north side of the city, near the zoo! Near Paul Kruger Street."

"Hang on, boys and girls," Nellie said, handing Amy back her phone. "Gomez and Cahills go Boom."

Boom Street ringed a large field across from the zoo. At the corner of Paul Kruger, Nellie hung a tight left turn, tires screeching.

A traffic sign on a wooden horse said:

DANGER: CONSTRUCTION SITE

HARD HATS* ONLY

At the bottom, scribbled in nearly illegible handwriting next to an asterisk, were the words *and Cahills*!

"Drive around it," Dan said. "They're up ahead."

Behind the sign, the street dropped off into a steep decline. Parked at the bottom was the purple pickup. Uncle Alistair stood beside it at attention, his cane in hand and his bowler hat neatly on his head.

Nellie put the car in first gear and rode the brake downhill. At the sound of the engine's whine, Alistair looked upward and waved them over.

"Alistair *is* working with the Holts," Amy hissed.

"He looks worried about something," Dan said.

"Be careful," Amy replied.

As Nellie slowed, Alistair's waving got more urgent. "Um, guys, what's with his hat?"

Two blue wires extended from the back of Alistair's bowler all the way into the driver's window of the pickup. Amy couldn't see anyone inside the cab, but Alistair was looking agitatedly across the street.

There, standing near a thick, gnarled acacia tree, were Eisenhower, Mary-Todd, Reagan, Madison, and Hamilton Holt, along with their pit bull, Arnold. Eisenhower leered triumphantly, his neck the color of rare roast beef. In his hand was a long yellow string leading to Alistair's bowler. "Let's talk," he said.

"Let's book!" Dan said.

Nellie threw the car into reverse.

Alistair's face turned ashen. "No, *don't*!" he shouted. "Retreat is not—I repeat, not—recommended!"

Eisenhower barked. "If you value human life."

"Don't listen to him!" Amy said. "Go, Nellie, go!"

"Ten-HUT!" Eisenhower held up his hand. "Your uncle is attached by means of technology learned and perfected by myself in Explosives Lab 101, Instructor Todd Bempster, West Point Class of None-of-Your-Business, to the pickup battery, in a manner too electronical to explain in civilianistic terms but easy to set up with the help of a few handy household—"

"Cut to the chase, will you, lamby?" said Mary-Todd.

Eisenhower held up the string with a triumphant smile. "If the hat comes off Alistair's head, the pickup explodes."

"He's bluffing," Dan said shakily.

"He's not." Amy knew Eisenhower meant business. And she liked the idea.

NOW you'll finally feel what our parents felt, Uncle Alistair. You'll know what it's like to be abandoned, instead of the one who abandons.

"YOU IN THE YUGO—COME ACROSS THE STREET, IF YOU KNOW WHAT'S GOOD FOR YOU," shouted Eisenhower. "ON THE DOUBLE!—ER, TRIPLE!"

Amy took a deep breath. She tried to grab on to a coherent thought in her brain, but they were flying around inside, slippery and dark like bats.

Dan put his hand gently on her shoulder. "Follow me."

He stepped out of the car and walked downhill toward the Holts. Amy followed behind, numbly. On the other side of the street, she could sense a change in the faces of Reagan and Madison—something like relief. This scheme, Amy realized, wasn't their idea. Hamilton was looking downright panicked.

She tried to meet his glance. He was blinking fast, as if he were embarrassed or fighting back tears. She felt a surge of gratitude toward him. For saving her life. For helping them against Alistair. "Ham . . . ?" she said.

Eisenhower clapped a beefy hand on his son's shoulder, nearly knocking him over. "We know you're here for the Tomas clue."

"We are?" Nellie blurted out.

Madison rolled her eyes. "Oh, *that* was convincing."

"Actually," Reagan murmured, "it was."

"When we heard you were going to Peoria on that intercept from Indonesia," Eisenhower said, "we made sure to follow."

"You mean, Pretoria," Nellie corrected.

"My husb—er, *we* bungled the flight booking," Mary-Todd said. "The two choices were so close on the drop-down menu. You see, by getting it wrong, we got it right."

"You found us by mistake?" Amy said. She glanced at Dan, but he was staring intently ahead, as if hypnotized by something.

"Who are you here to meet?" Eisenhower demanded.

"Reagan did some research?" Madison said, parking her gum under her tongue. "She found out that the Tomas have a clue? It has something to do with some South African tribe?"

"But if it's a Tomas clue, don't you know it?" Dan asked.

"You little brat," Eisenhower said. "Just like the others. Laughing at us. Looking down their noses. Cutting us off from the family secrets."

"Sweet pea . . ." Mary-Todd said. "Your blood pressure . . ."

The angrier Eisenhower got, the redder his face became. He clenched his fist around the string. Amy thought she could hear a frightened *yeep* from Alistair.

"Don't!" Nellie shouted.

"Who is your contact?" Eisenhower demanded. *"Where is the Tomas clue?"*

Stay calm, Amy commanded herself. She was shaking.

She looked at Dan. He seemed paralyzed, staring intently ahead.

"Your uncle's hat," Eisenhower said in a tense, measured tone, "is connected to a wire via a magnet, which creates a groundified circuit. Knock off the hat, the circuit breaks. The pickup—*bang!* And for good measure, a loose wire falls upon the base of Mr. Oh's brain. Five hundred volts. I would hate to see that happen on a beautiful day like this, wouldn't you?"

Suddenly, Dan snapped out of his trance. *"I know the clue!"* he blurted.

Amy spun around. "You *do*?"

Her brother was jerking his arm back toward the car. "I—I need to get the map. Permission, sir?"

Map? Amy stared at him in utter confusion.

"Granted!" Eisenhower barked. "And you know what happens if this is a trick."

Dan ran to the Yugo. He was sweating. His fingertips shook. He opened the passenger door and leaned in.

"Mrrp?"

Saladin mewed hungrily from the backseat.

"RAWRF!" Arnold lunged forward. His leash flew out of Mary-Todd's hand.

"No-o-o-o!" Amy cried out. *"Shut the door, Dan!"*

Dan scrambled to turn around. He pulled himself fully into the car. As he slammed shut the driver's door, Arnold banged headfirst into it.

The Yugo rolled downhill, toward the pickup.

"Pull back the handbrake!" Nellie shouted, racing toward the car.

"The *what?*" Dan said.

"He's heading for the pickup!" Reagan shouted. "Stop him!"

"No . . . oh, please, no . . ." Alistair murmured, his face puckered and sallow.

"THIS IS NOT ACCORDING TO PROTOCOL!" Eisenhower bellowed.

Hamilton Holt sprinted across the road. He pulled open the pickup's front door and dived inside, his fingers working a tangle of blue wires in the dashboard.

The Yugo was picking up speed.

"The lever in the center!" Nellie shouted. "Pull it!"

Hamilton leaped out of the cab. He leaned toward Alistair, turning his back, then whirled around.

The Yugo was fifteen feet away . . . ten . . .

"Now!" he shouted. *"Stop now, Dan!"*

Amy heard a metallic ratchet noise. The Yugo skidded left, turning sideways in the road.

She watched in horror as its right rear fender smacked against the pickup.

"DAN!" she cried, racing toward him. . . .

Her brother was trembling. Staring at the steering wheel of the stopped car.

In one piece.

Hamilton, Nellie, and Amy converged at the side of the Yugo. "I reset the mechanism," Hamilton said. "It's on a timer now. Three minutes. Take this. Go."

He handed Amy a folded-up sheet of paper and sprang away, running across the street. *"Move!"* he shouted to his family. *"It's about to blow!"*

The Holts all ran in the other direction. Out of the corner of her eye, Amy could see Alistair crouching behind a tree. When the Holts were a half block gone, he began limping away, fast.

Amy felt a hand on her shoulder. Dan was pulling her into the car.

The door shut and Nellie tore away as the pickup blew.

CHAPTER 14

Amy flinched at the sound of the bomb blast on Boom Street. Nellie was speeding the Yugo onto the highway entrance ramp.

"Yeeee-HAHHH!" Dan screamed, hitting the car roof with his fist.

Amy's insides were frayed. "You think that was *fun?*" she blurted. "We could have all been killed—because of you! *What did you think you were doing?*"

"Didn't you see him?" Dan said. "Hamilton—he was blinking!"

"So?" Amy said.

"Blinking Morse code, Amy!" Dan explained. *"Dit-dah-dit, dit, dit-dah-dit-dit, dit, dit-dah, dit-dit-dit, dit, dah-dit-dit-dit, dit-dah-dit, dit-dah, dah-dit-dah, dit!* Two words—*release brake!* He was giving me instructions."

"You understood that?" Nellie said.

"At first I'm, like, dude, what?" Dan said. "But he kept repeating the same message. He wanted me to create a distraction!"

"Are you crazy?" Amy pressed. "What if Hamilton

hadn't been able to fix the wires in time? You hit the van, Dan! *You hit it! A distraction doesn't mean dying!*"

Dan deflated. His face darkened, and he fell back heavily into his seat. "You really know how to ruin a nice day."

The car fell silent as Nellie pulled onto the highway and zoomed toward Johannesburg. "So, campers," she chirped, "what say we celebrate our escape, Alistair's escape, Hamilton's good-guyness, and Dan's great code-breaking skills by stopping off and getting us a fresh GPS? And maybe, like, some food?" She paused while Amy and Dan shifted uncomfortably. "I knew you'd jump on that idea. I'll keep an eye out for a place."

As the flat, parched countryside raced by, Amy stared out the window. "I wonder where he is now — Alistair."

"I saw Hamilton whisper something to him after he fixed the wires," Nellie said. "Must have been telling him to make like a tortilla chip and break away."

Dan shook his head. "I can't believe that wacko was going to zap him."

Amy closed her eyes. The plan was so barbaric.

Zap. One flip of the bowler.

She suddenly had the urge to cry.

Something was bubbling up inside Amy, something so muddy and deep she couldn't define it. "I . . . wanted him to die, Dan. I never felt that before. What's wrong with me?"

"Hey, kiddo . . ." Nellie said gently.

Dan nodded. "Yeah. It's understandable. Really."

THE VIPER'S NEST

83

"Is it?" Amy said. "*I* don't understand it. You should climb around inside my brain, Dan. It's like this dark room surrounded by quicksand."

"I know what you mean," her brother said quietly. "I hate being in my brain sometimes. I have to get out."

"What do you do?" Amy said.

Dan shrugged. "I go to other places—my toes. My shoulders. But mostly here." He tapped his chest and immediately turned red. "I know. It's stupid."

"Not really," Amy said. "I wish I could do that, too."

"It's not something you *do*," Dan said. "I mean, something's always going on in there whether you want it to or not. You just have to, like, lift up the shades and peek in."

Amy took a deep breath. The idea sounded so *Dan*. She closed her eyes and thought about the past few days. About Alistair and the hunt. About Dan and his body travel.

Lift the shades . . .

The quicksand was fading away. Relief washed over her. And she began to cry. "I hate myself," she said. "I hate what I'm seeing."

"Why?" Dan asked.

Stop feeling relief! she scolded herself. *Relief is weakness. Relief is compassion. Compassion is trust.*

Trust no one.

"Why do you have such stupid ideas, Dan!" she blurted.

Dan smiled. "You *do* feel happy, right? About Alistair?"

"I shouldn't!" Amy willed back the tears. "I can't! He always escapes. Mom and Dad didn't escape, but he does. It's not fair. He deserves to die."

"Amy?" Dan said.

"I don't want to feel glad that we saved Alistair!" Amy said. "Because saving him is like betraying the memory of Mom and Dad."

Dan nodded. He fell silent for a long time and then finally said, "You can't help it, Amy—being glad he's alive. I think Mom and Dad would be proud of you. They valued life. It's what made them different from some of those other Cahills. And Madrigals."

Amy thought for a moment. He was right. Being like a Madrigal was the worst possible fate she could imagine.

Sometimes—just *sometimes*—Amy wanted to put her arm around her brother. But the last time she'd done that, he'd washed his shoulders off and written CP on his shirt for Cootie Protection. So she just smiled and asked, "How do you know, Dan? You were so young when they died. Do you really remember them?"

"Not in my mind," Dan replied, gazing at the passing scenery. "But everyplace else . . ."

"*Turn left, now . . .*" said a soothing voice from the Yugo dashboard.

"Thank you, Carlos," Nellie replied with a grin. "I'm going to marry Carlos. I tell him what to do, and he just does it. No complaints."

Nellie's new GPS device, which they had named Carlos, was leading them into the city of Johannesburg. In the near distance, a cluster of glass-and-steel skyscrapers sloped up gently toward a slim, graceful structure like a giant scepter.

Amy's face was buried in a book. She had been reading aloud from it, a fact that made the trip seem about fifteen hours long. "'The N1 Western Bypass is part of a road system that rings the city, the busiest section of road in South Africa,'" Amy recited. "'As you approach Constitution Hill, notice the Hillbrow Tower, one of South Africa's tallest structures, resembling a more modest version of the Space Needle in Seattle.'"

"Uh—Amy?" Dan said. "We're *here*. We are *in* the traffic. We can *see* the tower."

Amy ignored him. "Let's find the Jan Smuts exit."

"Sounds like one of Nellie's boyfriends," Dan said.

Nellie leaned over and smacked him. "I'm loyal to Carlos. And he will find the exit for us."

"Smuts—pronounced *Smoots*—was an Afrikaner military leader and prime minister of South Africa," Amy said. "He supported apartheid, the separation of races. But in 1948 he came out against it—and lost the election. Can you believe it? I mean, the Africans—the ones who were here first—were treated like that? And you could only be president if you agreed to it?"

"They could have voted the bad guys out," Dan said, "like we do in America. Well, sometimes."

"We're not so squeaky clean," Nellie said. "My dad—

Pedro Gomez — was chased out of this town in the 'burbs? They hated Mexicans gathering on the street — but they were just waiting for farmers to hire them for daily work! My grandmother? She was going to settle in the South, until she saw this sign on a water fountain that said 'Coloreds Only.' She wasn't sure if she was or wasn't. But just the idea that she had to think of it was disgusting. Dude, why do you think there were marches and protests in the fifties and sixties?"

Dan recalled all pictures in textbooks and on a million PBS specials Aunt Beatrice used to sleep through. "People were crazy back then," he said.

"Crazy is something you can't help," Amy said. "This was planned. South Africa had always separated races, even in colonial days. Tribal people couldn't go into white cities after dark. They had to carry passes, or they were jailed. But apartheid didn't even start, officially, till, like, the forties. You had to be labeled black, colored, white, Indian. 'Colored' meant you looked part white, part black. If you weren't white you couldn't vote. You had to live in segregated areas — like our Indian reservations but called *Bantustans.* You had your own schools, doctors, and stuff — totally inferior. The government made Bantustans separate countries, so they could control people with immigration laws. You had white bus stops and colored bus stops. You couldn't marry out of your race."

Dan's head was spinning. This somehow didn't seem real. It didn't match what he was seeing outside the car window. But when Amy was on a roll like this, she had the facts locked.

Colored?

"How could you tell if someone was, like, colored?" Dan asked. "What did that mean?"

"They had tests," Nellie said with a shrug. "Like, looking at your skin color with paint samples? I don't know. Sometimes two people in the same family were called different races. So they had to move. Dude, people protested all the time. The Soweto student uprising in, like, the seventies? Kids were killed by police. Nelson Mandela? He was in jail for almost thirty years. He nearly died."

"Mandela's like this big honcho," Dan said. He could picture the guy on news reports, all smiley and kind-faced like your favorite uncle.

"Now he is," Amy said. "The government woke up. Foreigners stopped investing in South Africa. Protests were ruining the country. Apartheid ended, but not till 1994."

Dan looked out the window. He was feeling sick but not from the car. *Different countries for different races . . . police killing kids . . . 1994?* It didn't seem real.

He saw people of all colors heading out of buildings, leaving work. Some had heads down, some were on cell phones. If it weren't for the weird languages, it could have been home.

As the Yugo puffed up a hill, he saw a strange collection of buildings and a sign welcoming them to

Constitution Hill. The building on the left was sleek and modern, with a glass tower rising out of the center. A wall near the entrance contained the words *Constitutional Court* in different colors and languages.

Nellie parked, and she and Amy went straight to the court entrance, a massive carved wooden door. But Dan stood staring to the right, at another set of buildings, dirty and flecked with peeling paint. A decrepit lookout building sat above a thicket of razor wire, straddling two of the larger buildings. It was balanced precariously, as if a shove in either direction could send it tumbling.

"Sorry, miss," he overheard a guard saying to Amy, "Shaka Zulu died many decades before the prison was built. There is no connection to Shaka here. But of course you are welcome to come inside to see the museum."

"Come on," Amy said, grabbing Dan's arm.

Dan fell in behind her and Nellie. "Great. A museum next to a prison in the wrong town. That's a good start."

"Ssshhh," Amy said. They stepped into a cavernous, light-drenched foyer with slanted columns and colorful mosaic walls. "There's a library here. I saw signs."

"Whaaat?" Dan shot back. "The guy said *prison*, not library! Oh, I forgot. Same thing."

Amy took a left, then followed signs down a long hallway until they emerged into a towering room with a wide spiral staircase. "May I help you?" asked a woman with light brown skin and salt-and-pepper hair. She was wearing a simple string of white pearls that somehow seemed to pick up the tint of her deep brown eyes.

Amy wondered if her skin shade would have been considered "black" or "colored" in apartheid South Africa and immediately felt embarrassed. "Hi I'm, um, Amy and th-th-this is my b-b-brother, Dan, and N-Nellie," she said.

"We're looking for, like, Shaka Zulu information?" Dan said. "Also ice cream. If you have it."

"Americans—how delightful." The woman smiled and extended a hand. "I am Mrs. Winifred Thembeka, and I'm the librarian here. This is mainly a place for information about human rights. Alas, I'm afraid we don't have much about Shaka, although they're planning an exhibit for two years from now."

"Two years?" Dan said.

Mrs. Thembeka gave a sympathetic nod. "Our main reading room is on the third floor, should you care to use it. Ice cream is sold in the café."

"Thank you." Amy pulled Dan toward the stairs.

The third floor contained an airy reading room leading to endless stacks of books. "I thought this was a center for *human rights*," Dan said, shaking free of Amy's grip. "Now what? We look up every book about Shaka and hope we find a clue?"

"Have faith," Amy said, sitting at a computer terminal and typing in Shaka's name.

Nellie sighed. "I hope you're right, Amy. 'Cause Little Mister Ben and Jerry's here has a point. I mean,

I love you and all, but I'm thinking that at this rate we're going to end up living in this library."

Dan sat at another terminal, ready to start his own search. A glossy Constitution Hill pamphlet rested on the keyboard, and as he pushed it aside, he glanced at its title: "The Shameful History of Number Four."

Shameful History. That had some potential.

He began reading:

To understand the history of the South African people, their grit and defiance against oppression, we start at the Old Fort Prison Complex, also known as "Number Four."

Originally called Mentonville, it opened in 1893 on what was then called Hospital Hill. A fort was built around it several years later, after British uitlanders (outsiders) tried to overthrow the Boer government. At first, the prison housed only white prisoners. "Number Four" was built as a so-called "Native Prison" for blacks. Informers had their teeth yanked out. Some wore them around their necks. Built for 356 prisoners, it soon housed over 1100. Gangs of inmates often attacked each other. Flush toilets were not introduced until 1959. Striking mineworkers, victims of petty apartheid laws, "Pass Law" protesters, rebelling students of the 1976 Soweto uprising — all were kept in Number Four, as well as many heroes of the Congress Movement, including Nelson and Winnie Mandela, Albertina Sisulu, and Oliver R. Tambo.

Dan stopped reading. *This* was how they treated people under apartheid. What a waste of human life at Number Four!

Number Four.

Dan's mind flashed to the handwriting at the bottom of the Shaka card.

BIMRSESOSEIM GEKK #4

"Amy!" he blurted out. *"Number Four* — remember? It was written after the name we decoded? Number Four is also the name of the Old Prison!"

Amy bolted over. *"Constitution Hill, Number Four* — that's it, Dan!"

Dan went on reading, this time aloud:

"'The notorious prison has had its share of historical figures: Mahatma Gandhi, for protesting the condition of Indians; Winston Churchill, held here while a war correspondent before being transferred to prison in Pretoria. Although Churchill wrote publicly about the Boer War in his books *London to Ladysmith via Pretoria* and *Ian Hamilton's March*, a hidden trove of private correspondence about Number Four was found recently in Pretoria. Most of the papers were instantly stolen, but one of the only remaining documents was given to the Constitution Hill library as a bequest from the private collection of the late Mrs. Grace Cahill. . . .'"

Dan stopped reading. The silence on the third floor was total, as if even the air-conditioning ducts and computer electricity had shut down. "Grace . . ." he said.

"Dan . . ." Amy said. "That second name? The other Gekk brother? Do you remember what it decoded to?"

Dan remembered. "Church Hill . . ." he said. *"Churchill!"*

"Typo," Nellie said. "Should be two Hs, not three."

"Churchill was a Cahill," Amy said. "A Lucian."

"And the document was from Pretoria — as in 'Marching to Pretoria,'" Dan said. "The song Irina quoted? It pointed to where the document *was*. But Grace got there first!"

Dan typed in the name WINSTON CHURCHILL. A list of documents appeared, each with a line of identifying text. Dan looked for the one that said "gift of Mrs. G. Cahill" and pressed a button marked ACCESS.

The screen instantly turned blue:

PRIVATE HOLDING

NOT FOR PUBLIC VIEWING

CHAPTER 15

Dan's patented *I'm just a cute, curious kid* expression always got him results. "Can we just see that Churchill document?" he asked Mrs. Thembeka, with Oscar-winning innocence. "It would be, like, so cool to touch something that Churchill personally wrote."

He turned to Amy for support, but she was barely paying attention. Her nose was in a biography of Winston Churchill that she had found.

Mrs. Thembeka's phone started beeping, and she turned to pick it up. "I'm dreadfully sorry, dear, but our private holdings have very strict access. Excuse me."

"Nice try," Nellie muttered.

Dan's eyes wandered over to the file cabinets in the library office directly behind Mrs. Thembeka. The papers had to be in there. He looked around frantically for anything that he could use to help distract the librarian. But his eyes locked on a bronze plaque hanging directly over the file cabinet:

The Constitution Hill Library
Is Grateful for the Support
Of Our Generous Patrons to the
Literacy Campaign

* * *

Ruth Aluwani
Oliver Bheka
Piet Broeksma
Grace Cahill

"Amy, look!" Dan blurted out. "Grace! She's all over this place."

Mrs. Thembeka glanced up at Dan. She murmured something into the phone, hung up abruptly, and came out from behind her desk. "Did you know Grace Cahill?" she said. As she looked from Dan to Amy to Nellie and back, her eyes misted. "Oh, my goodness, I should have known. You look just like her."

"I do?" Dan said. He adored his grandmother, but she did have silver hair and wrinkles.

"The eyes are the same. And you . . ." Mrs. Thembeka took Amy's hand. "You must be the beloved grand-daughter of whom she so often spoke. Please, sit." She gestured toward a chair and a small sofa and went to shut the office door. "I was so sorry to hear of your grandmother's passing. We were good friends, you know. How did you find this place? Was it Robert?"

Dan looked at Amy. "Uh, we don't know any Robert."

Mrs. Thembeka reached inside her desk, pulled out a stack of old photos, and held one toward them. "You see? This was, oh, ten years ago."

In the photo, Mrs. Thembeka and Grace stood arm in arm under a theater marquee, on which could only be seen the words *by Athol Fugard*. Grace's skin was quite tan. In fact, her skin color was nearly identical to Mrs. Thembeka's. "You look like sisters," Amy said.

Mrs. Thembeka laughed. "Perhaps we were. In our souls we were very much the same."

Dan flipped the photo and saw a faded inscription:

Lemur by day . . . Aloes by night . . .
Fine adventures, dear friends!

He held it toward Amy, who looked as if she were about to cry. "Lemur . . ." she said. "That must be *The Flying Lemur*, Grace's private plane."

"We'd had a full day of flying that afternoon — oh, did she love that airplane! Swaziland, Banhine National Park in Mozambique, refueling . . ."

"What's 'Aloes'?" Dan said.

Mrs. Thembeka smiled. "A reference to the play we saw, *A Lesson from Aloes*. The aloe plant thrives under the worst imaginable deprivation — harsh sun, no water for months. It is a symbol of the South African people, surviving despite apartheid. Some aloe species have quite remarkable healing properties. Grace loved this play."

"How did you know her?" Amy said.

"She was on the library board committee that interviewed me," Mrs. Thembeka said softly. "They were about to hire a more seasoned administrator, but Grace insisted on someone passionate about human rights. I'd been involved in the struggle since my cousin Vuyo's . . . experience. He was a student in Soweto. . . ."

Was.

Mrs. Thembeka's voice trailed off, and Dan recalled what Nellie had said about the Soweto uprising.

Kids were killed by police.

He had to turn away.

"Can I look through these?" Amy asked, gazing at the pile of photos.

"Of course, dear." As Amy eagerly took up the photos, Mrs. Thembeka unlocked another desk drawer. "A few months ago, Grace left me a phone message. She sounded weak, but I had no idea she was dying. She alerted me about the Churchill document. She said I was to list it in the catalogue but limit it strictly to scholars and her direct descendants. With positive identification." Mrs. Thembeka shrugged, looking a little embarrassed. "It was an odd request, something we weren't used to — frankly, I don't imagine any library would be. But she was insistent. Because she had done so much for us, the board approved. So, although I hate to ask, I will need to see proof. . . ."

"I think I have my school ID." Dan fumbled in his pocket. He pulled out a crumpled Mars Bar wrapper, some loose string, a cherry Starburst, several unidentified pieces of clear plastic, and his dad's Australian passport. He panicked for a moment, until he spotted a corner of his school ID jutting out from it.

He opened the passport and laid it flat. His ID was sticking to an inner page. He peeled it off to reveal his dad's passport photo and fake name, Roger Nudelman. "Here you go!" Dan said, holding out the ID.

But Mrs. Thembeka was riveted on the photo, her eyes widening. "Nudelman . . . ?" she said. "What on earth are you doing with Nudelman's passport?"

"Oh," Dan said. "That's actually not—"

Amy stomped on his foot under the desk. Dan was about to whap her upside the head, but he caught her glance and instantly read what was behind her eyes. *She obviously doesn't know Dad, and there must be a good reason for that*, they were saying.

"He's my . . . find of the month," Dan ad-libbed. "The passport was on the floor at the airport."

Dan thought he could see Mrs. Thembeka shudder. "Then I would destroy it," she said. "And if you were to find his wife's, destroy that, too. Although it probably wouldn't help. Forging passports is nothing to murderers and thieves."

CHAPTER 16

Murderers? Thieves? *This has got to be a mistake.*

The names on the passports had seemed a little odd to Amy, but not familiar. Maybe Dad had chosen a South African crook's name by mistake.

Amy glanced at Dan, but he was staring at the photo. "I—I don't think—" he stammered.

"Honestly, I can't imagine how this passport ended up on the airport floor," Mrs. Thembeka said as she opened a file cabinet. "The Nudelmans were Aussies, I believe, but they went all over the world on their spree. India, Indonesia, South Africa . . ."

India, Indonesia, South Africa . . . Arthur and Hope's route in pursuit of Amelia Earhart.

"What did they do?" Nellie insisted.

"Without using graphic details," Mrs. Thembeka said, "suffice it to say, brutal crimes with no motives. Ransacking buildings and leaving no one alive. Happily, they haven't been seen in years. I assumed they'd died, but . . . ah, here we are!" She lifted a document from the file and put it on the desk. "You may copy it, if you promise to keep it to yourselves."

"But — about the —" Dan began.

Amy cut him off with a strong glare.

A mistake. That was it. Pure and simple.

"Thank you," Amy said. "We'll make a copy."

Dan ran out of the building. He was trembling.

"Wait up!" Amy said, clutching a manila envelope.

Nellie followed close behind. "Dude, you're shaking," she said, putting a hand on Dan's shoulder.

"Sorry!" Dan took a deep breath. "It's just . . . she called them . . . murderers."

"She's old. Bad eyesight," Nellie said reassuringly.

"Wouldn't Mrs. Thembeka know what Dad looked like if she and Grace were good friends?" Dan asked.

"Like I said, *old*," Nellie said. "Grandparent-old. People like that don't show off pictures of their grown-up children. That's, like, for parents of little kids."

"So . . . Dad chose to use the name of a *famous bad guy* on his passport?" Dan asked. "Why?"

"Maybe he didn't know who Nudelman was," Amy said. "'Roger Nudelman' — that's the kind of goofy name Dad would always make up. Remember Oscar Schmutz, the dirty-fingernail wizard?"

Dan shook his head sadly. "No."

Amy fixed her eyes on Dan's. "What *do* you remember about them, Dan — Mom and Dad?"

"Practically nothing," Dan said, his eyes welling up.

"Dan, think," Amy said. "You told me you didn't remember them in your mind, but you did everyplace else. What were *those* memories?"

Dan was breathing hard. "Silly stories. Hot chocolate on the white kitchen table. Songs at night. This clean-laundry smell. Big arms around me . . ."

"When you were about two," Amy said, "I heard Dad say to Mom, 'I just want to reach forty-three. Then he'll be eight, and if I die, at least he'll remember who I am.' I wasn't supposed to hear it, and it scared me. Mom told him he was being morbid. I'll never forget what she said next. 'Babies remember souls, Arthur.' So for a year or so I tried to put you near Dad's shoes. I thought she was saying *soles*. Okay, I figured out what she meant — but it wasn't until now that I really understood. Those things you remember? *That's* what Mom meant. "

"People like your mom and dad," Nellie said gently, "are not capable of such bad things."

"Irina turned out to have a good soul," Dan said. "And she was capable of very bad things."

Amy put her hand on Dan's shoulder. "Irina found her goodness late. Mom and Dad already had it."

"Right," Dan said. "That's true. Can we go now?"

As he walked to the car, he unfolded the copy of the Churchill letter.

Amy linked arms with Nellie. She hoped Dan could let go of this. She hoped she could, too.

In the parking lot, Dan laid out the copied letter on the backseat. "Check this out . . ." he said in awe.

FROM THE DESK OF
WINSTON LEONARD SPENCER-CHURCHILL

11 May 1900

My Darling M____ C____,
      Tho' my loyalty to Britain &
taste for tumult may have drawn me
to the Anglo-Boer conflict eventually, I
commend you for urging that
my war reporting begin here now.
My loss in the election, as you say,
was a scar to be borne bravely &
is surely meant to strengthen me,
as will our army's troubles with the
mighty Boers strengthen it. Yes, I
did escape imprisonment from Pretoria's
State Model School, to where they'd
taken me (fortunately!) from H. Hill.
One cannot summon words for that
filthy pit in Johannesburg, a place
far more miserable than my fetid
hidey hole in Witbank's mines, post-
escape (where I was able indeed
to discover a realization, given herein!).

This I send you,
With all my heart,
Your Winnie

The unbroken line shall deliver
thy desire to the letter, if thou
proceedeth downward ever,
in single steps.

"This is a big help," Dan said disgustedly.

"H. Hill," Amy said, flipping through her Churchill biography. "That must mean Hospital Hill. That's what they used to call Constitution Hill back then."

"Right. And Churchill hated it." Nellie shrugged. "No big shocker there."

"It says here that Churchill was taken from the prison here and transferred to a place called the Staatsmodel, or State Model School, in Pretoria," Amy went on.

Dan nodded. "Where he wrote this. Where it stayed for years until Grace sent it to Constitution Hill."

Amy continued reading her book. "Okay. They were using that school in Pretoria as a prison. Churchill scaled a ten-foot wall and escaped to a mining town called Witbank, where he hid until he was able to hop a supply truck. It all checks out with the text in this letter!"

Dan leaned close. "What's this bit at the end? 'The unbroken line shall deliver thy desire . . .'?"

"An unbroken line could mean, like, eternity," Amy said, scanning her book's index.

"Or a circle," Dan suggested. "Or a box or a trapezoid or any kind of closed shape!"

Amy glanced at the top of the letter. "Who is M-blank C-blank?"

"C for Cahill!" Dan blurted out. "Maybe he was writing this to, like, our great-grandmother. Do we know her first name?"

"No," Amy said, pacing back and forth. "Okay, let's think this through. The guy at the airport gave us the code that led us here. Somehow, he's connected with all this. Grace left a secret document here for us, a document stolen from Pretoria and written by a Cahill.

The Holts have reason to believe that there's a Tomas clue hidden somewhere in South Africa—"

"Yes—and Churchill knew what it was!" Dan said. "That's what Grace is trying to show us. Maybe the location of the clue died with Churchill. Look at what Old Winnie wrote at the end of the message."

"'Witbank's mines . . .'" Amy read, "'where I was able indeed to discover a realization . . .' A Cahill writing to possibly another Cahill about *discovering a realization*! Sounds like a clue to me."

Amy felt light-headed. Grace was talking to her from the grave—did she know where the Clue was?

Nellie slid into the Yugo and began tapping her new GPS. "Carlos, darling, take us to Witbank."

It took longer than expected to find Witbank, mainly because its official name had been changed to Emalahleni and no one had told Carlos. No one had told Carlos he should be an air conditioner, either, and as far as Dan was concerned, that was even worse.

After a few confused questions in a petrol station, they were driving toward the abandoned mine where Churchill had been hidden.

Amy was reading again. Constantly.

"'. . . a town built on its rich mining resources, Witbank was the home of British sympathizers who hid Churchill after his daring escape from the State Model School . . .'" Amy read.

"This was before he turned into . . . you know, a famous fat guy," Dan said.

"Prime Minister of England," Amy corrected. "During World War Two."

Nellie parked in a small lot. A house stood nearby and behind it a parched landscape marked with mounds of dirt. They walked through the open door.

Inside the building, a craggy, thin man with a pencil behind his ear played chess with a teenager.

When the guy turned around, Amy began stuttering. Silently. It was a feat only Amy could manage, and only Dan could notice.

And it only happened in front of boys who looked like this one. He had brown hair and caramel-colored eyes, like Dan's friend Nick Santos, who made all the sixth-grade girls turn into blithering idiots when he looked their way—in fact, would even say *Watch, I can make them turn into blithering idiots,* and then he'd do it. Only older.

"He. Is. Hot," Nellie said under her breath.

"You too?" Dan hissed.

"Checkmate!" Mr. Hottie exclaimed.

"Wowww," Amy managed.

"Um, we're looking for the Churchill escape site?" Dan said.

The man groaned and rose from his chair. "It's out back. You'll see the plaque. Help 'em, will you, Kurt? We'll have our rematch when you get back from chorus rehearsal tomorrow."

The boy smiled—mostly at Amy.

"Sorry, her heart belongs to Ian Kabra," Dan said, except that something in her expression made him realize her heart didn't belong at all to Ian right now.

Kurt gave a perplexed smile. "Walk this way," he said, unfolding himself to his full height, which had to be at least 6'2". Amy watched him swagger to the door.

"Churchill hid from the Boers in this mine shaft after his escape," Kurt said, "until he was smuggled out in a supply truck."

"Did he, like, leave any messages here?" Dan said. "You know, letters written to someone from inside the mine? With stuff about, um, locations and stuff?"

Kurt leaned closer to Dan. "Sounds like you know the secret — that the Churchill story was all a lie."

"Yes, exactly," Dan said, playing along and trying not to look like an idiot. "A total lie. I knew that."

"A l-l-lie?" Amy squeaked.

"Churchill was a double agent," Kurt whispered. "That's why he was in South Africa. Not to be a reporter. To find secrets."

"A double agent for the Boers?" Nellie asked.

"Someone else," Kurt said. "Some group. He left a symbol on a clothing scrap we have inside. Two snakes and a sword, with a big L. Haven't figured it out yet. But he was looking for something. And he was exchanging messages with his agents, in the tunnels. I know, because he left a message on the wall."

Dan glanced at Amy and knew she was thinking that same thing he was. *L — Lucian.*

"What did it say?" Dan said.

Kurt shrugged. "I saw it when I was a boy. I used to spend hours down there, practicing my singing where no one could hear me." He smiled at Amy. "I used to be shy."

"Where's this wall?" Dan demanded. "Can we see it?"

"You have asthma," Amy said. "Mines are dusty."

"So was the cave in Seoul," Dan said. "I was fine!"

"Well, take a look," Kurt said, gesturing toward a rickety structure, a fenced-in area marked OFF-LIMITS. "There have already been a few incidents with that mine. Look at the thing the wrong way, and something inside collapses. They plan to cave it in soon."

"So . . . we can't get inside?" Dan said.

"Sure, if you're looking for a free burial," Kurt replied. He winked at Dan, then turned to Amy. "Do you play chess?"

"A l-l-little," Amy stammered.

Perfect. Dan couldn't believe his good fortune.

"She's great," Dan said. "She'll kill you!"

"I accept the challenge," Kurt said flirtatiously. Dan couldn't believe it — did Kurt actually *like* his sister?

Red-faced, Amy followed Kurt to the building. And Dan backed slowly away.

Toward the abandoned mine.

CHAPTER 17

"Are you out of your mind?"

Dan spun around. In the setting sun, he saw Nellie in silhouette. With her current hairstyle, she looked like a tiny stegosaurus mounted on a human body. "He winked," Dan said. "Meaning it's okay to do this."

"You *are* out of your mind," Nellie said. "He winked because he likes your sister. Amy is being held captive by the mad chess fiend of South Africa."

Dan looked over her shoulder. Through the window he could see the older man was chatting, fixing something on a stove, while Amy and Kurt sat playing chess. When they weren't looking at the board, they were sneaking glances at each other.

"They're perfect together," Dan said. "And he was exaggerating about this mine. These guys get all nervous about this stuff for insurance reasons."

"Do you even know what that means?" Nellie asked.

"No," Dan said. "But hey, it's been here since the eighteen-hundreds, right?"

Nellie thought a moment. Then she reached around,

unhooked her backpack, and pulled out a flashlight. "Take this. If I hear one pebble come loose, I pull you up for safety reasons. Duck down into the shaft. Do not fall. If you find something written on the wall, I will help you write it down. If you don't, that's it. We're out of here. Got it?"

Dan grabbed the flashlight. "You are awesome."

"I know. Now hurry."

Dan ran toward the shack and darted around back. In the center of a fenced-in area was a wide hole with the top of a frayed rope ladder bolted to the rim. He gulped. "This ladder is looking a little vintage."

Nellie peered over. "Okay, Plan B. You lean over and look. That's it. I'll hold your legs. Hurry!"

"Right." For a moment Dan froze. The last time he was in a mine, in Coober Pedy, Australia, he had encountered poisonous spiders and a deadly snake. Not to mention asthma. *You're not actually going in*, he told himself. *Just dipping down a little.*

Swallowing hard, Dan got on all fours at the edge of the hole. He could feel Nellie's hands gripping his ankles as he flicked on the flashlight.

The hole was wide enough for one person. The walls were slick, as if painted with shellac. The rope ladder hung down, disappearing into nothingness and swaying slowly on the current of some invisible breeze. An acrid, vaguely rotten stench wafted upward.

My fetid hidey hole in Witbank's mines . . . Churchill had written.

"What do you see?" Nellie hissed.

"Hold tight," Dan said.

The rock walls were rough and pocked, and a jagged crack ran down the opposite side. Dan thought he could spot some writing, but it was just the accumulation of gravelly dirt on a narrow ledge.

"I hear something!" Nellie said. "Make it fast!"

Nada.

Dan exhaled. It was too dark, too much pressure. "Beam me up, Scotty," he said.

The words caught in his mouth. His flashlight was angled inward now, shining on the wall just below him.

And there, carefully carved into the rock about four feet directly underneath him, were several lines of writing. *"Wait! I got it!"* Dan cried. "Lower me a little! I see something!"

Nellie inched forward. Dan sank lower into the shaft. Pebbles shook loose from the rim and rained downward into the hole — into silence. Dan never heard them reach bottom.

Dan squinted, reaching down with the flashlight to the writing on the wall. It was too hard to read.

A rubbing. That would do the trick.

"Pull me up!" Dan said.

In a moment, Dan was over the edge of the hole. "Okay, Nellie, I need to go back down, this time with a sheet of paper and pencil. There's writing down there, and I can get it by rubbing it."

"Now I *know* you're crazy," she said.

"Checkmate!" Amy's voice echoed from the hut, followed by a laugh from the old man and a playful moan from Kurt.

"We have a few more minutes," Dan said. "He's going to ask for a rematch."

"How do you know?"

"It's a guy thing!"

Nellie sighed. Rummaging around in Dan's pack, she pulled out a pencil and a notebook, ripping out a sheet. "Okay, but be quick."

Maneuvering the light, the pencil, and the paper wasn't going to be easy. "I'll need spares," he said. "In case I drop something."

With a look of exasperation, Nellie tore off more sheets and found two other pencils. Dan stuffed them into his pants pocket and held on to the originals.

Clasping the flashlight in his mouth, he said, "Chhochhay, chech go!"

Dan stretched out on his stomach at the hole's edge. He felt a shudder and heard the sound of pebbles slipping down the wall beneath him. He moved left, until he gripped what felt like solid rock.

"Chhere!" Dan said, inching over the edge.

"Just a minute, dude, you have something sticky in your pack," Nellie said. "I'm getting it off my—"

Suddenly, the ground beneath Dan fell in an explosion of black soil. He felt himself drop abruptly. And then he was hurtling down into the darkness, his mouth open in a silent scream.

"GOTCHA!"

"YAAAAGH!" Dan thought his left leg was going to be pulled out from its socket. He was hanging by it, with Nellie's hand clasped around his ankle.

His arms flailed. Pen and paper fell. The flashlight flung away, casting a wild, brief light show around him.

"I'm pulling you up!" Nellie called.

Dan instinctively pressed his hands against the wall, looking for a root, something to support him, just in case.

The wall was solid here, filled with tiny cracks.

No. Not cracks.

Carvings.

"I got it!" Dan said. "I got the message!"

"You're heavy!" Nellie complained.

"One minute, Nellie! Just one minute!"

Quickly, he pulled the spare paper and pen from his pocket. He placed the paper over it and began to trace.

When he was pretty sure he was finished, he folded the paper and tucked it back into his pocket. *"Okay — now!"*

"Arrgghhhh . . ." Nellie pulled. Dan felt himself begin to rise. Slowly.

He felt a jolt. Soil poured down around him, catching in his hair, sliding into his upside-down pants. "Pull harder!" he yelled. "It's collapsing!"

"I'm pulling as hard as I can!"

Now Dan could hear a commotion. Other voices—Amy's, Kurt's, the old man's.

He felt himself rising steadily. He tried to grab on to the wall but it was slipping out beneath his fingers wherever he touched it, sliding down in cascades of soil.

"Yeeee-ahhh!" came Kurt's voice—and Dan was rising over the top, coughing.

"Hhhhhhh . . . hhhhhh . . ." His breaths were contracted wheezes, papery-sounding in the night.

"Bring him inside!" the old man's voice said.

Asthma. Sometimes, in emergencies, adrenaline kicked in and prevented the symptoms. The way it had happened in Seoul. But asthma was unpredictable. And now he felt as if someone had put a cloth over his nose and mouth.

He felt himself being carried inside and set down on a sofa. "Chew on this," Kurt said, handing him a tube-like, cactus-ish object, broken to release a white liquid.

It tasted bland and oozy. Dan gagged at first but forced himself to swallow. Amy sat by his side until he was breathing easy again.

And *then* she freaked.

"How could you have done that?" she said, then glared at Nellie. "And *you*—you're supposed to take care of us, not encourage Dan's stupid ideas!"

"But—" Dan sputtered.

Amy wasn't letting him have a word. *"Don't you get it? We're all we have, Dan! Just you and me!"*

"I—I found Churchill's message!" he said.

"You *what*?" Kurt said.

"You *what*?" Amy repeated.

Dan reached into his back pocket and took out the rubbing. "It was on the wall of the mine shaft!"

"*Ex*-mine shaft," Kurt said. "A big sinkhole of rocks and soil now."

"A sinkhole!" Amy echoed.

Kurt lifted a powerful flashlight from a window ledge and shone it out over a section of sunken earth.

"I — I would have been buried in that?" Dan said.

"Don't think about that, my friend," Kurt said. "Let's have a look."

Dan glanced at his sister. "Aren't you going to repeat what your new boyfriend said?" Before she could react, he spread out his wall rubbing on the table:

AM LOST, TIRED, GONE IN, DRIVEN NOUGHT WE HIT A SHARK — O CONFUSED LETTERS, FLEE, LOVER, FROM THESE LINES!

WLSC -29 086341 3132817

Dan stared at it in silence, reading it over and over.

"WLSC . . ." Kurt said.

"Winston Leonard Spencer-Churchill!" Amy added.

"You guys make a great team," Dan remarked. Once again, Amy blushed.

The old man was beaming. "Will you look at that! We didn't even know he'd been hiding in *that* shaft!"

"Well, some of us did," Kurt murmured. "But . . . what does the writing mean? It's completely daft. Like the ravings of a madman."

"Word," Nellie agreed. "The dude was shut up for weeks in a mine shaft. Who wouldn't go a little postal?"

Kurt burst out laughing. "'We hit a shark'?"

Churchill going postal. Madman. Daft ravings.

Dan did the only thing that made sense.

"Yeah, you're right," he said, holding up the sheet. "Total nonsense. Let's forget any of us ever saw it."

As Amy and Nellie stared, open-mouthed, he ripped the secret message into small pieces.

CHAPTER 18

Amy couldn't believe it.

Something had happened between her and Kurt. She couldn't really explain it. Yes, they'd played chess. But there had been more to it than that. Like her senses had all been suddenly plugged in.

For the first time in weeks, she had been able to think about something other than the hunt.

Then, just like that, she had to go.

There was barely time for a good-bye.

"Good luck," Kurt had told her.

But all she felt was the bad luck of the moment.

And then there was Dan's destruction of Churchill's message.

"How could you do that?" she asked as Nellie sped them away from the Witbank mine . . . and Kurt.

Her brother looked at her in disbelief. "Come *on*, Amy. You didn't think that just because I ripped it up —"

"I know, I know, you memorized it!" Amy said. "It's the Dan Cahill Mental Gymnastics Show. But that's not the point! How could you have taken that incredibly stupid risk in the mine? You could have died! Again!"

"I found what no one else has found in a hundred years," Dan said, "so maybe you say, like, thanks?"

"He also tricked those two guys into thinking the paper meant nothing," Nellie said.

"You're just as bad as he is!" Amy shot back.

Dan held up a finger. "Winston Churchill once said, 'In wartime, truth is so precious that she should always be attended by a bodyguard of lies.'"

"How do you know that?" Amy asked.

"It's right there, on the page your book is open to," Dan said, pointing to the biography on the car seat. "Churchill was all about hidden messages. He worked with spies. I locked this baby in my head, dude."

On the other blank page Nellie had given him he wrote out what he had found in the mine:

AM LOST,
TIRED, GONE IN,
DRIVEN NOUGHT.
WE HIT
A SHARK

—O CONFUSED LETTERS,
FLEE, LOVER, FROM THESE LINES!
WLSC
-29.08634/ / 31.3287

"Churchill wasn't crazy," Dan said. "And he wasn't drunk. I'm betting this all means something."

Amy stared at the words. "'We hit a shark'?"

"I'm buying the nutcase scenario," Nellie said.

"Okay, okay, it sounds a little weird, but let's think," Dan said. "Isn't that what you do when you're attacked by a shark—hit it on its snout?"

"Churchill just escaped from prison, right?" Nellie said. "So maybe it's some English expression for victory. Like, 'Ho-ho, we really hit a shark there, didn't we, old chap?' Very Kabra, don't you think?"

"Dan?" Amy said. "Remember that code we had to solve on Uncle Alistair's estate, to open the hatch in his backyard? Where the hint was actually a play on words? What if this thing is actually two parts—the top part is the code, and the bottom part is the instructions for decoding it?"

"Hmm . . ." Dan looked at the last few lines of the message. "So, 'O confused letters' would be part of the instructions."

"Yup, and 'confused' could be a code for 'scrambled.' Scrambled letters means an anagram," Amy said. "And 'flee'—that means the same thing as 'leave' in Uncle Alistair's puzzle. You have to take something away, like a letter or word . . ."

"Lover!" Dan said. "That's it. He doesn't mean a real lover. He means the word *l-o-v-e-r*! And 'from these lines'—five letters, five lines!—wait, I think I know . . ."

AM LOST, – L = <u>AMOST</u>

TIRED, GONE IN, – O = <u>TIREDGNEIN</u>

DRIVEN NOUGHT. – V = <u>DRIENNOUGHT</u>

WE HIT – E = <u>WHIT</u>

A SHARK – R = <u>ASHAK</u>

Dan slapped his forehead. *"Agggh*, it's in *Dutch."*

"I don't think so," Amy said. "Churchill was a Brit, not a Boer. So now we unscramble. Okay, that second to last word is easy — *with."*

"Shaka!" Dan blurted out. "That's the last word! So the final words are *with Shaka!* Okay, I'll get the rest of it in two minutes. Time me. Go ahead."

But Amy was staring at the first word already. "Dan, I think we hit the jackpot."

Dan's face lit up, the way it did whenever the supermarket stocked Red Sox ice cream. Slowly, he attacked the puzzle and didn't stop until he'd finished:

<u>AMOST</u>   TOMAS

<u>TIREDGNEIN</u>   INGREDIENT

<u>DRIENNOUGHT</u>   IN THE GROUND

<u>WHIT</u>   WITH

<u>ASHAK</u>   SHAKA

"Tomas ingredient in the ground with Shaka!" Dan blurted.

"That was three minutes seven seconds," Nellie remarked.

"He knew!" Amy said. "Churchill knew the location of the Tomas clue!"

"He must have found out while in prison," Dan said. "Or maybe there was a Cahill running the mine."

"So . . . the clue must be buried with Shaka's corpse," Amy said.

"*Now* we're talking!" Dan replied.

"Ew," Nellie called from the front seat. "We have to dig up a body?"

"Dan?" Amy asked. "Where is Shaka buried?"

Dan took out his Shaka book and leafed to the end. "Well, no one is one hundred percent sure. But legend has it he was killed in a place called Durban, which is in the KwaZulu-Natal province."

"Which is, uh, where?" Nellie said.

"Past the Mpumalanga province," Dan replied.

"Thanks a lot."

But Dan was looking at the bottom of the code sheet. "One thing. What about these lotto numbers?"

Amy looked at them closely. "They look like longitude/latitude coordinates. Can we find out where it is?"

Dan began fiddling with the GPS. "Have Carlos, will travel."

The phone rang just as Professor Robert Bardsley was listening to the final strains of the Mahler "Resurrection" symphony. "Oh, dear, Winifred?" he said, wiping away a tear as he picked up the receiver. "You caught me at an emotional moment."

As he listened to the voice at the other end, his tears dried. He turned off the music. "You met who? Yes, I know she had grandchildren—how old?—that's wonderful. How sad she's gone. So you showed them the Churchill letter? Aha . . . yes, I don't know why the secrecy, either. A rather tepid love poem, if you ask me. Oh, I'm sure they are remarkable children. *Pah*, not to worry, neglecting to give them my contact info was fine. Why would they want to meet a tired old academic like me? Thank you for the call . . . tea indeed, perhaps when I'm in Joburg in July. Yes, good night."

Hanging up the phone, Professor Bardsley packed a few CDs, a telescope, a pitchpipe, and a set of infrared glasses into a canvas bag and peered out the front door. The street was clear, as far as he could see. But he would need to take precautions.

He ducked back in, dialed a number, and reached voice mail. "Hello, Nsizwa, this is Bardsley. I will need you to take over rehearsal tomorrow morning, as I have been called away for the day." Pausing a moment, he added, "Come to think of it, I may need the group. You shall hear from me soon. . . ."

On his way out, he lifted a floppy hat from atop his closet shelf, and a hunting knife.

CHAPTER 19

"Ending a sentence with a preposition," said the official at the Shaka Museum in Durban, "is something up with which I shall not put!"

"Say what?" Dan was not in the mood for this. The ride the previous night had taken hours. And now, after a few hours sleep in Durban, the center of the KwaZulu-Natal province, and a trip to the museum, all he had asked for was the bathroom. Not a grammar lesson.

The guide smiled. "You are Churchill people, no? You don't recognize your hero's quote? He was famous for saying it to someone like you. You said, 'Where's the bathroom at?' This is ending a sentence with a preposition! Very bad!"

"Um, I gotta go, Mister . . ." Dan said.

"Cole," the man said. "First door on your right."

On the way in, Dan nearly collided with an ancient guy whose face was nearly skeletal. "Sorry, dude."

When he was finally relieved, Dan skipped back outside. The old man, moving very slowly, hadn't even made it across the room.

"Over the years, from time to time," Mr. Cole was saying to Nellie and Amy, "some people have inquired about the relationship between Churchill and Shaka Zulu. Father doesn't like those visitors very much." He gestured toward the old man.

"Well, Churchill couldn't have had a relationship with Shaka," Amy pointed out. "He was born almost fifty years after Shaka died."

"Indeed," Mr. Cole said. "We told this to our visitors time and again. Then, one day, after a visit, one of our prized possessions disappeared—a very large shield that belonged to Shaka. My father was on duty at the time, and he has never forgiven himself."

"The shield these guys took?" Dan said, pulling his Shaka card out of his pocket and turning it toward the man. "Did it look like this?"

Mr. Cole nodded. "Very much so."

"And this group—did they happen to be, like, big?" Dan asked. "And, like, loud and bossy?"

He couldn't help noticing that the old man had almost reached them. The man was scowling, and when he spoke, his voice was a whispery rasp. "Why do you want to know about Churchill?" he demanded.

"Father, please, these are children, not thieves." Mr. Cole smiled apologetically. "My great-grandfather— my father's grandfather—knew Churchill."

"Churchill was *sneaky*," the old man said. "Obsessed with Shaka. That is why he traveled to South Africa. Not to report. Not to fight. To find out about the *isipho*."

Dan glanced warily at his sister, then back at the old man, whose eyes were reddening. *"Isipho?"*

"It is something Shaka gave to the Europeans," the old man said. "They saved his life with their medicine, and he thought they had magic powers. But they were looking for something, too. Something the Zulu had. Something the Europeans took and transformed into a potion. It was said to have magnified his powers."

Amy's eyes were saying exactly what Dan was thinking. *Sounds like Cahills.*

"A p-potion?" Amy asked.

"Nonsense, of course!" the old man shot back. "But they said Shaka could be one of them — their family. Shaka trusted them! He should have trusted no one! Shaka should have given Fynn the *aniklwa*!"

"Father, please, let us not start again," Mr. Cole said. As he led his father back to the exhibit, he gave Dan an apologetic shrug. "Feel free to explore."

"The Tomas!" Amy said as Nellie turned onto the highway. "That's who Mr. Cole was talking about."

"Big meatheads asking about Shaka and Churchill," Nellie said. "That'd make sense."

"And stealing a shield that just happened to have the Tomas crest on it," Dan remarked, his nose buried in his Shaka biography.

"Remember what Mr. Holt was whining about," Amy said. "The other Tomas finding the clue, blah blah

blah? I thought he was being paranoid, but maybe he was right. Maybe the thieves who visited this museum were the ones who eventually found the clue."

"Fynn — okay, here he is!" Dan said, pointing to a page in the Shaka biography. "This is the guy the old man was talking about — Henry Francis Fynn. After a battle, he gave Shaka medical help and weapons. Shaka was so grateful he allowed the Brits to hang out in the Zulu kingdom. Then things started going bad. Way bad. Years later, Fynn was dissing Shaka in some book. Saying he was a monster."

Amy nodded. "England was trying to colonize South Africa, mostly because of the diamonds."

"Right!" Dan said. "And anyway, even without the European rifles Shaka was a superstar. Before him, tribes would throw long spears at each other and wait. Like, ho hum, arrow arrow in the air, hey, want some coffee? Shaka said no way, José — well, maybe not José but the Zulu equivalent — short spears are better! Then you can go right up to your enemy's ugly face and *wham! Stab! Arrrrgghh!*"

"Have you considered a writing career?" Nellie said.

"Does your book say what an *isipho* is?" Amy asked.

"Negatory," Dan said, shaking his head.

"Dan . . ." Amy said. "Fynn and the other Europeans . . . they told Shaka he was *one of the family.* That's what the old man said. Maybe Shaka *was* a Cahill after all. Not by birth, but because of something they exchanged. The *isipho.*"

Following Carlos's guidance, Nellie drove out of Durban going northwest toward -29.086341 / 31.32817. Small villages dotted the countryside, each a cluster of circular mud-brick huts with tightly thatched roofs. In one village, a group of men herded cattle into a rickety wooden pen. In another, Dan exchanged waves with a team making bricks out of mud, stacking them in perfect red-brown piles. Nellie had to swerve to avoid a group of women walking along the road, each balancing what looked like an entire tree's-worth of branches on her head. And an outdoor classroom of small children looked up idly as the Yugo passed, just as bored as American kids.

"Road not detected," Carlos was saying now. "Make a right turn when possible."

Nellie stopped. To their right was a crowd of people spread out among blankets covered with clothes, beads, crafts, and containers of food. Around the perimeter people sang and danced, children ran around playing games, and older people sat like kings and queens as the others rushed to entertain and feed them. Most of the villagers wore everyday Western-type clothing, but a few were dressed in colorful feathers, calfskins, and beaded dresses.

"A street fair," Dan said, "without the street."

"*Sawubona!* Welcome!" one of the vendors called out, a young man dressed in what looked like leopard skin, complete with a leopard headband. He gestured to the bounty around him and spoke in a clipped, heavy accent that sounded vaguely British. "We have beads, statues, food! Join us! I am Mondli—*Mondli*, the Zulu word for one who feeds! And you?"

"Dan," Dan said. "The American word for one who eats. What's the occasion?"

"Pension day! The elders in our community receive pay every month. And we respect our elders. So we celebrate, and they buy!" Mondli let out a laugh and then held out an elaborate beaded skirt toward Amy. "For the young lady?"

"It's more . . . Nellie's style," Amy said.

But Nellie was looking off into the distance. "Um, guys? According to Carlos, we're going there."

Dan followed her gaze. Beyond the fair, a sloping field rose steeply upward, dotted with rugged rock formations. At the top, a distant herd of long-horned antelopes grazed quietly. A wooded area stretched down a slope to the left. But Nellie was looking at a squat white building at the top of the hill.

"There?" Mondli said. "Are you certain? May I ask, what business do you have?"

"We're . . . um, researching Zulu culture," Dan said. Amy shot him a *lame-o* look.

"Ah, well, in that case, stay with us here," Mondli said. He gestured toward the hill and frowned. "The people who built this place are not Zulu."

"Who are they?" Dan asked.

Mondli shrugged. "White people, yellow people, dark people — a factory. They told us they would bring jobs. But the people who went to work there — they changed."

"Changed?" Nellie said. "In what way?"

"Secrets," Mondli said with disgust. "They never would tell us. Very important. They said our people will benefit, but we have not seen that. Some of our young men and women disappeared. The company said they have been transferred. To secret locations."

One of the elders, who had been sitting close by in a beach chair, now walked toward them. He was barefoot and wearing plain, loose-fitting clothes. "*Tokoloshe!*" he said, a shaky finger pointing up the hill. "*Tokoloshe!*"

"Excuse me." Mondli nodded respectfully and escorted the man back to his chair, speaking to him in Zulu. As he walked back, he gestured for Dan and Amy to follow a bit farther away. Under the shade of a tree with a canopy that looked like someone had pressed it flat with a giant hand, Mondli said, "We have been trying to get these people to leave the community. I am a university alumnus, and a group of us are working with someone there. We have not been successful." He glanced up the hill. "We do have a spy within, but to achieve anything against these people, you practically need an army."

Dan was not liking the sound of this. He gazed up at the imposing building and swallowed hard. "If we, um, decide to go up there, what's the best way?"

Mondli pointed out a route up through the steep incline among the rocks. "I don't suggest it, but . . . stay on the pathway. Whatever you do, avoid the trees. There are hunting traps." He stepped back, pulling a sheaf of papers from underneath his robe. "I am a cartographer by trade. My firm is involved in mapping the area. We are not quite finished, but here is a copy. For a souvenir."

"Thanks." Dan nodded. "One question. What was that old guy telling us?"

"He is a *sangoma*, a traditional healer," Mondli said. "Most people look up the hill and see a big company. He sees something else. *Tokoloshe*."

"*Toko . . . ?*" Amy said.

"There is not a word in English for this," Mondli said with a sigh. "Perhaps you believe in a soul? The *tokoloshe* take the soul away. They steal it, and it never comes back."

CHAPTER 20

GUARD DOGS

LIVE ELECTRICAL CURRENT

ALARMED!! KEEP OUT!!!

Dan gaped at the sign over the locked gate. Behind it was a stone walkway flanked by shrubbery. It led to a windowless building with six sides, constructed of pale marble that seemed to change shade as you walked. On one side, a massive air-conditioning machine hummed, and over the front door hung a sign with a corporate logo: UBUHLALU ELECTRONICS.

"Well, that's cheery," Nellie said.

"I—I think Mr. Mondli was right," Amy said. "We probably shouldn't do this."

"How would we get in?" Nellie said.

"Do we want to get in?" Amy asked. "This could be a wild goose chase. I mean, Churchill wrote those coordinates over a hundred years ago. We don't know if the Tomas are really here. What if they moved on?"

Nellie glanced skeptically at the building. "This place doesn't look very Tomas-ish," Nellie said.

Dan thought for a moment. Churchill had given coordinates for a Tomas clue. Mr. Mondli's description made it sound like these people *could* be Tomas. But companies could be unfriendly, too. "Let's scope the place out," he suggested, heading around the side of the building, "and be careful in the bushes."

"Why?" Amy said.

"This is South Africa, dude," Dan replied. "Where cobras come from. And not the hot ones, like Ian."

He followed the building to its opposite side, where a hill sloped gently downward. Extending from the back of the building was an ugly, rusted metal structure that looked like the remains of an old warehouse. Above it rested sheets and sheets of sleek blue solar panels. A tidy white picket fence enclosed the warehouse, extending from the larger building's wall down the hill. A weary-looking gardener was opening a door in the warehouse. He scowled, waving for them to go away. Then he disappeared inside.

"Green recycling," Amy remarked. "Old building on bottom, solar collector on top."

Attached to the fence was a sign with a message in different languages. In English it said DO NOT PROCEED BEYOND THIS AREA/ENERGY COLLECTORS.

"Okay, that does it," Nellie said. "I say we head back down the hill, buy some beads from the locals, crack a few antelope jokes . . ."

But Dan had his eye on something. A vertical wooden post was attached to the bigger building, with a glass strip running down its length. A series of these posts, like stray cacti, had been placed in the grassy area between the picket fence and the solar collectors—like the remains of an older fence within the newer one. "Amy, do you have any coins?"

Amy pulled out several Indonesian *rupiah* coins from her pocket, which she gave to Dan. Rearing back, he tossed them toward the old building.

Dzzzit! Dzzzit! Dzzzit! Dzzzit!

One by one, they sparked and fell to the ground, trailing wisps of smoke.

"Who-o-oa," Nellie gasped. "What'd you do?"

"It's an invisible electric eye," Dan said. "Go past it, and you're nuked. The gardener must turn it on and off."

"Nuking people to protect solar panels?" Amy said.

"Come on, let's pay these guys a visit." Dan began sprinting back to the main entrance.

Amy caught up to Dan in front of the warning sign. "'Guard dogs . . . live electrical current.' Who goes first?"

"Maybe there's a doorbell," Nellie said.

"Hey, this could be worse," Dan said. "At least it doesn't say . . ." Out of the corner of his eye, he spotted a slithery movement in the grass. *"SNAKE!"*

Amy rolled her eyes. "Very funny."

"No, Amy, look!"

"Ghhh . . . gchhh . . ." The words caught in Amy's throat. She felt the weight across her shoe tops even

before looking down. When she did, her feet were under the flowing green body of a snake at least six feet long. It slithered fast, its eyes wide.

"*Mamba*," Dan said, remembering it from science class. Snakes were one of the only topics that kept him awake in school. "Don't. Move. As long as its head is close to the ground, you should be all right."

Amy's arms were vibrating. Her face was bone white. The bulk of the snake's body was over her now . . . the tail . . . almost gone . . .

THWACK!

The building's door swung open. Amy jumped.

With an angry hiss and a flare of its sides, the snake reared up out of the grass.

"Dan!" Amy yelled.

A man stormed toward them, down the flagstone walkway. He was dark-skinned and close to seven feet tall, with a potbelly that strained the buttons of his black shirt. A scar split his left eyebrow, running down his cheek to his jawbone. He glared at them with bloodshot eyes. In his right hand was a rifle.

The snake rose higher, eyes now on the guard. As the man approached, it lunged forward.

With one fluid motion, the man lifted a stick from the ground in his bare hand. The mamba clamped its teeth down hard on the stick. Calmly, the man tossed the stick down the hillside, the snake flailing along with it.

He glared at Dan, Amy, and Nellie. The anger in his eyes had turned to puzzlement. "May I help you?"

On his badge was the name A. Bhekisisa.

"Th-that was awesome," Dan said.

The guard smiled. "Thank you. I am confused. An alarm went off. Was that you?"

"Maybe," Dan said. "We got kind of lost."

"We're . . . l-l-looking for our p-p-parents," Amy stammered.

Dan groaned inwardly.

Mr. Bhekisisa laughed. "I'm so sorry. The gun is making you nervous. I carry it by orders. We have some sensitive and very expensive equipment here. People are always trying to steal. Come!"

Amy hated the place. It was vast and clean, with polished floors and rubber-wheeled vehicles scuttling to and fro. Around the perimeter were cubicles where geeky-looking people were scrolling through spreadsheets.

Mr. Bhekisisa asked them to empty their pockets for security, apologizing the whole time. He offered to dispose of Dan's candy wrappers. He looked at Amy's various folded notes and souvenirs. He fiddled with Nellie's iPod. Then he opened their backpacks.

Irina's wallet.

Amy froze. If he looked inside it, he'd suspect *something.*

But all he did was stir everything around and hand the packs back. "So sorry, they are quite paranoid here," Mr. Bhekisisa said. "So. Where are your parents?"

"We're, um, early," Dan blurted out. "They should be here in an hour or so."

"Then I will take you on a tour," said Mr. Bhekisisa.

As he walked ahead, Dan muttered, "Killer electric eyes, for *this*?"

"I think I know what the *sangoma* meant," Nellie said. "This place does take your soul away. Yuck."

Amy passed a wall lined with cartons partially hiding a door marked with a small sign:

RADIOACTIVE: AUTHORIZED PERSONNEL ONLY

Her eyes stopped. Where did the door lead?

She took a mental map of the room.

The solar-energy storage area. The old warehouse.

The door was about where those outbuildings had been. She examined the sign.

Radioactive.

That was weird. Solar energy wasn't radioactive.

Then again, solar energy wasn't usually protected by an invisible high-voltage fence.

She crept closer. The door had a small, shiny, rectangular panel near the latch. On a hunch, she pulled out Irina's wallet from her pack. She flipped through the plastic ID cards until she came to Reagan Holt's. Carefully, she held it up to the panel.

A small LED screen lit up:

HOLT, R.

PLACE FINGER IN SENSOR NOW

CHAPTER 21

"Dan, you have to come now! Nellie, too!"

Amy raced into the Ubuhlalu Electronics employee lounge, looking unbelievably excited.

"Where *were* you?" Nellie blurted.

"Don't tell me," Dan said. "You found a library."

"Where's the guard?" Amy said, looking around.

Dan gestured toward Mr. Bhekisisa, who was standing in a corner, talking into a cell phone.

Amy grabbed Nellie's hand. "Quickly!"

Dan followed them across the floor. Amy led them to a door hidden behind a stack of boxes. He leaned in toward the door's sign. "'Radioactive'?" he said. "This should lead outside, to those buildings."

"Exactly," Amy said. "Okay, remember Irina's wallet, with all the IDs? She had one for each of the Holts." Looking left and right, she pulled out three plastic ID cards, one each for Hamilton, Reagan, and Madison. "When I put Reagan's card against the screen on this door, her name registered."

"It's a Tomas hiding place," Dan said. "I knew it! And we have access!"

Amy shook her head. "It needs a fingerprint, Dan."

"Dang, I knew we should have amputated when we had the chance," Nellie said.

Dan frowned. "Wait — the door is just *here*? Unhidden?"

"If this company is a front," Amy said, "then there are a lot of Tomas here. Maybe everybody is. So hiding it wouldn't be necessary. People probably come in and out of this door all the time."

"Let me see that wallet," Dan said. Amy handed it to him, and he dug around, taking out the three small zipped plastic bags, each containing a microscope slide. On each bag, an initial had been written in black marker. Dan carefully opened the one marked H and took out the slide. He held it up to the light.

"It's impossible to see anything," Amy said. "Someone left a smudge smack in the middle."

Smudge.

Smudge meant handling. Handling meant hands. Hands meant . . .

"It's not a smudge," Dan said. He separated the two pieces of Plexiglas comprising the slide. Inside it was a moist, shriveled-up membrane in the shape of a cap. "It's a fingerprint."

"What?" Amy said.

Dan reached into the wallet again and extracted

Hamilton Holt's ID card. "Hold this," he said, handing the ID to Amy. As delicately as he could, Dan snapped the membrane cap over his right index finger. It felt a little slimy, more substantial than he expected.

He nodded at his sister. "Now."

Amy waved the card over the plate.

HOLT, H.

PLACE FINGER IN SENSOR NOW.

A round disk glowed red, just below the words. Dan pressed his capped finger to it firmly and waited.

"Nothing," he murmured. "What did I do wrong?"

He pulled it away to look at the membrane.

The red disk sputtered and turned green. The door emitted a beep.

CLEARANCE SECURED!

WELCOME, HAMILTON HOLT.

With a click, the door opened.

"Now, *this* rocks . . ." Dan said.

As he stepped onto an escalator, he turned toward Nellie and Amy. One by one, they had cleared the sensor. The door had sealed shut behind them and they were now in the connected building.

Like the tip of an iceberg, the solar-paneled structure was only the top of a gargantuan headquarters that seemed to stretch out forever. It was as if the entire hill had been hollowed out.

The place was alive with natural light. There must have been windows strategically placed among the solar panels—maybe even windows embedded in the grassy surface of the hill beyond.

As the escalator descended, Dan could see the arrangement of the place. It was shaped like a vast hive—interconnected hexagonal chambers with glass walls, each chamber filled with people.

The strangest part was the voices—grunts, cries of anguish, shrieks for mercy, triumphant bellowing. Like a torture chamber with an unlimited budget. Some chambers contained two people, some groups—wrestling, boxing, forms of combat he had never seen before. Some of the glass walls were smeared with red.

"What are they doing in there?" Amy asked, her face contorted in dismay.

"It's not ballroom dance class," Nellie said.

As the escalator reached bottom, a trim, gray-haired man bustled toward them. "Holt," he said, eyeing them impassively. "The United States?"

"Yes," Dan replied.

"Mr. Malusi," the man said efficiently. "Follow me."

"*EEAAARRRGHHH*—STOP!" a voice screamed as they walked past a chamber marked COMBAT FREESTYLE.

"It is quieter in my office," Mr. Malusi said over his shoulder. He led them into a spacious room, frigid with air-conditioning. He gestured toward a set of leather chairs as he sat behind a dark polished-wood desk. "Holt . . . Holt . . ." he said, fingers tapping on his phone. "Not much information here. Oh! Oh, my goodness. Ha! Eisenhower . . ."

Despite himself, Dan felt the pang of insult. "Our family has been loyal for generations—"

"Yes, yes, the sins of the father, et cetera," Mr. Malusi said, vaguely waving the thought away. "It is still very good you have volunteered for the training."

"Training?" Nellie said.

"You have seen our pods," Mr. Malusi said. "Each is dedicated to an aspect of Zulu training adapted for the twenty-first century—agility, tactics, strength, endurance. The Zulus, of course, were the greatest warriors ever known. Under history's greatest leader. We are a leadership school." He stood up abruptly. "We have exactly two hours for a tour and dormitory placement. Then you must choose your combat specialty."

"I—I—I don't know if . . ." Amy stuttered.

But Mr. Malusi was already out the door.

They followed him past a three-walled boxing ring where two men were duking it out with lightly padded gloves and no helmets. Each whirled with blinding speed, leaping impossibly high, lashing with legs and arms, seeming to defy gravity as they ran up the walls to execute flips and frontal attacks.

"Now, that's cool," Dan said.

"It is the art of *samhetsin*, a martial art invented by the Tomas," Mr. Malusi said.

Just beyond the ring, taking up nearly half the room, was a dirt-floored cage. In it was a bare-chested man facing a slavering animal with a sloped back.

"Is that a hyena?" Dan asked.

Mr. Malusi nodded. "Chosen for the power of its jaws, which can crush and pulverize bone."

The hyena leaped at the guy. With a grunt the man stepped aside, managing to avoid the animal and dart out his hand to its neck at the same time.

The hyena collapsed silently onto the floor.

"Excellent, Mr. Yaman!" Mr. Malusi called out. Noticing Amy's look of horror, he said, "Do not be concerned. Mr. Yaman has mastered the art of nerve isolation, which demobilizes the animal only briefly, before we let it back into the wild."

"And if he misses?" Amy said.

Mr. Malusi shrugged. "He doesn't."

As Mr. Malusi moved on, Dan felt Amy grabbing his shirt. "D-D-Dan, we can't do this," she said.

"I know," he whispered. "I'm thinking."

"Unlike the other branches," Mr. Malusi said over his shoulder, "we realize we are at war. Ownership of the clues will require the greatest defense, the fiercest and most skillful protectors the world has known. Other branches may have the technical know-how, the design skill, and so on. Only the Tomas will be prepared to keep and hold the secret of the thirty-nine clues."

And do what? Dan thought. *What exactly do you do when you find the greatest power on earth?*

Dan looked nervously at Amy. He could tell she was thinking the same thing.

"How will you—*we*—share it?" Dan asked.

Mr. Malusi turned, tilting his head curiously. "Share? That's an odd concept. Does a country share its nuclear stockpile? Does a successful merchant share his goods? We are not in the business of chaos, young Hamilton. We are in the business of taking and holding. For the benefit of our glorious family."

He led them to a section set off from the others, the size of several pods put together. "Our theater," he said. "Your timing is impeccable. The Shaka Zulu play begins in five minutes."

"Can I go to the bathroom first?" Dan asked.

Mr. Malusi looked at his watch. "Three minutes. Fourth pod to your left."

Amy had a creepy feeling even before the play began.

The Tomas training center was like being in some kind of end-of-the-world fantasy. Was *this* the branch philosophy? People turning into fighting machines? If this was what power did to people, why search for the 39 Clues at all?

Because Grace wanted you to, she thought. *She had a plan. And she was not a Tomas.*

Or was she? Amy realized that besides her and Dan, Grace was the only Cahill whose family branch she didn't know.

As the lights dimmed, Dan slid into the seat next to her and the play began. Mr. Malusi, who was sitting one row in front of them, looked at his watch and glared disapprovingly at Dan.

To the rhythms of a musical group in traditional dress, the play told the life story of Shaka. It was brutal and realistic, climaxing in the Ndwandwe-Zulu battle, with hundreds of actors sweeping away each other's shields with grand gestures, then driving spears into each other's chests. Amy closed her eyes.

"Ew," Nellie murmured.

"It's not real," Dan whispered. "I don't think."

When Amy opened her eyes, the actor playing Shaka was shoving a screaming older woman into a hut. Her face was covered in bluish-brown makeup, her eyes solid white. She was chanting to the heavens, causing a burst of stage lightning. From upstage came three realistic-looking, slavering jackals. Mr. Malusi turned in his seat to face them. "Shaka was great but ruthless," he explained eagerly. "He believed that the mother of Zwide, the Ndwandwe king and his main rival, was an evil *sangoma* whose spirit had magically entered the Zulu kingdom and slaughtered his people. So when he captured her, he fed her to the—"

"*AAAHHH!*" came a scream inside the hut.

Amy couldn't take it. She leaped up and ran.

"A Tomas with a weak stomach?" Mr. Malusi said to Dan. "We have training for this, too."

"I'll talk to her," Dan said.

He found her outside the theater, pacing back and forth. "Let's go," she said. "I want to get out of here, Dan. I hate this place."

"You are brilliant," Dan said, taking Amy by the arm. "I was trying to figure out a way to leave the theater with you, but you did it for me. Hurry."

"Where are we going?" Amy said.

"I wasn't in the bathroom," Dan said. "When we came down the escalator, I noticed a pod that was different than the others. So I went and looked at it. . . ."

He led her to the center of the hive. There, inside a chamber of ivy-covered glass walls ascending toward a skylight that seemed miles above them, was a sun-drenched quadrangle with grassy, twisting paths. Exotic cacti with brightly colored shoots obscured what looked like a stone monument inside.

"It's, like, two acres," Amy said.

"Come," Dan said. "We're allowed. We're Tomas."

Amy followed him into the huge pod and along one of the paths, until they were standing at the monument. It was shaped like a circular Zulu hut with a pointed thatched roof. In front was a statue of Shaka Zulu, holding a body-sized shield.

At the center of the shield was the Tomas symbol.

"This was the shield stolen from the Durban museum!" Amy whispered.

Dan was looking at a series of plaques on the walls of the hut, each in a different language.

"Dutch . . . Afrikaans . . . Zulu . . ." Dan read. "Xitsonga...Xhosa...Sesotho...Setswana...SiSwati... Shangaan . . . Venda . . . Tsonga . . . *English*. Okay. Read this."

IN MEMORIAM
Shaka Zulu
WARRIOR • UNITER
May His Soul Rest in Peace
But Live in the Freedom
Of South Africans Everywhere

"Dan, is this . . . ?" Amy asked.

"A crypt?" Dan's face was so alive with emotion it looked like it was going to crack. "Okay, this building is at the location of Churchill's coordinates—and he wrote 'Tomas ingredient in the ground with Shaka.' The legend says Shaka was buried in Durban, but no one has ever been able to prove it. *This is it*, Amy. We found the real burial place of Shaka Zulu!"

Amy looked down. The soil was dry and hard, the base of the monument choked with cactuslike plants.

When she looked up, Dan was holding a spear. "What are you doing with that thing?" Amy hissed.

"It's not a *thing*, it's an assegai," Dan said. "They're all over the place here. I hid one in the vegetation."

He pointed it toward Amy and plunged it down.

"Hey!" Amy shouted, lurching aside.

The spear sank with a solid *thunk* into the dirt, splitting a cactus plant. "I can do this," Dan said. "But I'll need cover. How long will that play last?"

"Mr. Malusi isn't going to be fooled for long!" Amy insisted. "This is suicidal. I am putting my foot down, Dan. This will not happen."

"Dan? Amy?" Nellie called out from the corridor. "Yo, where are you guys?"

Amy whirled around, and the door swung open.

CHAPTER 22

The man in black hated airports. So much waiting, so much security.

He looked up. His surveillance had indicated enemy arrival at any minute. But flights were crowded today. Schedules would be disrupted, landings postponed. They could be circling for a long time. Or, heaven forbid, sent to another airport.

But Lucians had a way of sneaking up on you, and the man in black was nothing if not patient. Out of the corner of his eye, he spotted someone approaching the circular landing pad. An airline employee. He lowered the magnification lens over his sunglasses and waited for a clear frontal view of the face.

There. Using the high-res telephoto cam in his glasses frame, he captured the image, uploading it to his portable surveillance device. He waited .7 seconds for a facial recognition check against the master database.

He was a Lucian operative. A Fixer, no doubt. Very well paid these days, as it had become so difficult to infiltrate airlines.

The man in black smiled. The two men were waiting for the same arrival. But for very different reasons.

A distant familiar noise cut through the airspace above. The Lucian lackey looked up, his face a rigid mask of efficiency.

As the man in black began to move forward, a large silk handkerchief came down from behind, in front of his face. His hand darted upward, catching the scarf before it could make contact with his neck.

Hermès. Silk.

Whirling around like a skater, the man in black lifted the scarf, and with it, the arms of his attacker.

He brought the scarf down around the neck of Alistair Oh.

"Arrrgglllchh . . ." Alistair sputtered.

"Alistair," said the man in black, "I would have thought that at your age, with your experience, you would know better than to make such a serious mistake."

Dan stood stock-still against the Shaka monument, holding his breath.

"Yo, Amy, Dan — Mr. Malusi is looking for you!" came Nellie's panicked voice from the direction of the courtyard-pod door. *"Where are you guys?"*

"I'll take care of this," Amy said to Dan. "I'll go back to the theater and make up some excuse to Mr. Malusi about where you are. Hurry!"

She ran to the door. With a soft *thump,* it shut.

Dan made a quick circle around the monument. Where to start? The cactuslike plants were thick and stubbornly hard to move. He yanked the stalks aside as best he could, examining the smooth stone at the base of the monument, hoping for some hint.

Just under the statue of Shaka, the stone was gouged in about three or four places, as if someone had banged it with blunt instruments. A thick shovel could have done that. It was as good a place as any to start.

Dan dug in with the blade. The soil was packed thick, but he hacked away, sending up little explosions of dirt. An assegai may have been a great spear, but it was a terrible shovel.

Outside he could hear a commotion, a rumble of voices. He plunged harder, a rhythmic *chuck . . . chuck . . . chuck . . .* echoing ever louder against the surrounding walls.

A voice filtered in from outside, growing closer. "I know he is only a boy—but he is a *Tomas* boy, and I expect a Tomas sense of responsibility!"

Mr. Malusi.

CHUCK . . . CHUCK . . . CHUCK . . .

Sweat dripped into Dan's eyes. It stung.

"Can you show me the women's m-m-martial arts?" Amy was saying.

THOCK.

Dan stopped and knelt. The arrowhead had hit

something solid. He brushed aside loose dirt. This wasn't a root or a rock. It was metal.

Dan placed a hand near the assegai blade and steadied the shaft with his other hand, scraping away the dirt until he made out the edges of a square.

He dug down the four sides. It seemed like he was cutting through more plant life than soil. The network of roots was so dense it looked like an army of dead snakes. Finally, he shook the thing loose and pulled it out.

It was a small metal cube, hinged halfway down and held shut by an ancient, dirt-choked lock.

Wiping away the soil, Dan saw the word *Shaka* carved into the face of the box. He tugged at the lock, but it wouldn't budge.

Dan's heart pounded. Churchill's message had said *in the ground with Shaka.*

This had to be it.

He stood, scraping the dirt back over the hole. He shoved broken plant shards over the mound, tamping it all down with his feet. Tossing the assegai into a thicket, he swung his backpack around and opened it.

Then he noticed the sharp ridge of the monument's stone base jutting about a half inch from the statue of the hut. If he could bring the lock down on that, hard . . .

Letting his open backpack fall to the ground, he held the box high over his head. He brought it down, but it smacked against the stone, resounding dully in the courtyard.

He gritted his teeth and lifted the box again. With a

loud grunt, he smashed it downward. The lock smacked against the edge and broke cleanly in two.

BWWWOPP! BWWWOPP! BWWWOPP!

An alarm sounded. Dan picked up the box and his pack and ran for the door. With a loud clank, it swung open.

Mr. Malusi barged in, with Amy and Nellie close behind. *"Young man, what on earth are you doing?"*

CHAPTER 23

"AMY, NELLIE, RUN!" Dan shouted.

Mr. Malusi was racing toward him. Dan ran to the assegai, picked it up, and threw it toward one of the glass walls. The spear pierced the network of vines, shattering the wall in a deafening explosion.

Dan ran to the wall at full speed, leaping around the plants. He jumped through the hole and out of the pod.

The vast central room, with its winding pathways between pods, was in chaos.

"STOP HIM!" Mr. Malusi's voice bellowed.

From the left.

Dan's eyes scanned the area, and he sprinted right, clutching his backpack. Amy and Nellie were running toward him now. "Follow me!" he shouted.

A loud thrum permeated the complex. Bright emergency floodlights flickered on overhead, circling columns of blinding white light around the rooms. On all sides, Dan heard the thumps of closing doors.

"The escalator!" Nellie said.

Dan glanced upward. The door above the escalator

had opened, and men in white suits were streaming in from the other building. "I don't think so," he said. "Come on. Let's move to the outer wall and follow it."

The dense network of overlapping pods made the wall the best place to hide. They crept slowly along it. In the chaos, Dan heard a high-pitched shriek above them. "Duck!"

They went down, but Dan realized it was a bird. It must have flown in through the gardener's door.

The door.

Where was it? He glanced around frantically.

There. It was shut tight, way above their heads. Next to it was a metal-mesh cage. An elevator cage. "Follow me!" he shouted, sprinting to the bottom of the cage. The elevator was resting on the floor, its door open. Inside were two broken clay flowerpots and sections of garden hose. "Get in!"

When Nellie and Amy were inside, he shut the door and swung a metal dial to the ON position. The elevator rose slowly above the chaos. They shrank down against the soil-encrusted elevator floor, out of sight, unnoticed by the swarms of screaming Tomas below.

"STOP THEM!" a voice bellowed.

Almost unnoticed.

The elevator suddenly stopped. *"Dan!"* Amy screamed.

The top ten or so inches of the elevator door had risen into the frame of the old warehouse exit. It was big enough for a human body. Dan yanked open the elevator door, then cupped his hands. "We can do this. Amy, you're first."

"I can't leave you!" Amy protested.

"Hurry, before they lower this thing!" Dan said.

He hoisted her up and she squeezed through the opening.

"You next, little guy," Nellie said. "And don't even *think* of arguing."

She boosted him through. Dan tossed aside his backpack, leaned in, and reached down for Nellie. Together he and Amy grabbed Nellie's arms and pulled.

The elevator creaked and juddered. It was sinking now. "PULL!" Nellie screamed.

She was halfway through, but the space was closing.

From behind them, a man's arm reached into the elevator opening. The palm pressed upward against the elevator's ceiling, while the elbow jammed against the ground.

The elevator groaned, then stopped moving. With his other arm, the man grabbed Nellie.

Dan stiffened. No time to wonder. No time to look.

"Heave-ho!" the man shouted.

"YEOOWWWW!" Nellie squeaked through, tumbling onto the grass.

Dan and Amy tumbled with her, as the elevator sank quickly out of sight.

"You dropped this?" a deep voice said.

Dan turned to face the man who had saved Nellie.

Mr. Bhekisisa held up the Shaka box. He was not smiling.

"Where did you find this?" Mr. Bhekisisa demanded.

"I didn't mean to steal anything. I'll give it back!" Dan said. "We—we can work this out together!"

"Come with me, all of you," he said. *"Now!"*

He began running down the hill, away from the front door of Ubuhlalu.

Amy had no intention of following this guy into . . . what? "Where's he going?" she asked.

"Do you need an invitation?" Mr. Bhekisisa said.

"Come on," Dan said. "He has the box!"

As Dan, Amy, and Nellie raced after him, Mr. Bhekisisa called out, "They have not had a security breach like this. You are lucky. I told them you had found the secret tunnel network. That will occupy them for awhile."

"Wait . . . you're—" Dan said.

We do have a spy within, but to achieve anything against these people, you practically need an army. . . . That's what Mr. Mondli had said.

"You're a spy!" Dan blurted.

Mr. Bhekisisa was moving fast. "I was . . . a Tomas," he said breathlessly. "Now . . . I am as I was born. A South African. Hurry. There are more of us waiting."

"More?" Nellie said. "How did they know?"

"Hurry!" Mr. Bhekisisa headed down the slope,

toward the woods. There, a group of men and women were trudging upward toward them.

Dan ran after him, with Amy and Nellie close behind. His eyes were focused on the man in front. He was instantly familiar, his face etched with wrinkles and a long scar, his eyes gray-green. His khakis and button-down shirt were a much tidier outfit than the peddler garb he'd been wearing before.

Do you need a car service? Or can spirited young people like yourselves navigate South Africa on your own?

"You!" Dan said. "You're the guy at the airport—the one who gave us the card!"

The man was wiping the sweat from his brow. "What happened up there, Bhekisisa?" he asked urgently.

Mr. Bhekisisa held up the box, smiling broadly. "They are very smart children."

The other man's jaw dropped. "Good God, have you really found the Churchill clue?"

"Your hint . . ." Amy said. "Constitution Hill . . ."

"Yes, and Church Hill," the man replied, his words clipped and quick. "Pardon my creative misspelling on that one—a bit of poetic symmetry. I am Robert Bardsley, professor of music. These are my students." He gestured behind him but kept his eye on the box.

Amy gasped. Dan jerked his head and followed her gaze toward the edge of the group, where a tall, brown-haired boy was standing, grinning.

"Kurt?" Amy said, her eyes widening. "What are you doing here?"

"I sing with Professor Bardsley's class sometimes. He said he was taking us on a field trip." As Kurt stepped forward, his eyes moved over to Mr. Bhekisisa, who was panting as he clutched the box. Kurt's excited grin faded into a look of concern as he turned back to Amy. "Are you okay? What's going on?"

Professor Bardsley clamped his hand down on Kurt's shoulder. "You children know Kurt? A fine singer — I only wish he could come from Emalahleni more often." He smiled at his student, then turned back. *The clue. Is it in there?*

Mr. Bhekisisa held out the box to Dan, who took it. "I will let the brother and sister have the honor. But we must move out of sight."

"Come, then," Professor Bardsley said. "Quickly."

He began rushing toward the trees. Kurt grabbed Amy's hand and followed, with Nellie on their heels.

But Dan froze. *Whatever you do, avoid the trees.*

"Wait — we can't go there!" he cried out. "Remember what Mr. Mondli said!"

"We can't worry about that now!" Amy shouted back. "These guys must know the area!"

Dan sprinted downhill and caught up to Nellie, Amy, and Kurt, who were running with Professor Bardsley.

"Who's chasing you?" Kurt said as he helped Amy over a fallen branch.

"She'll explain later," Nellie said breathlessly. "So, Bhekisisa is not a real Tomas. You guys are with Bhekisisa. You're here to rescue us. You know about the thirty-nine clues. And you're a professor who happened to be traipsing through the trees with his chorus?"

Professor Bardsley spoke fast, his eyes constantly darting back over his shoulder. "Most of us were once Tomas. We know the training pods. We know the townspeople here, too, and the way the Tomas have exploited them. I am a South African. I have long been weary of exploitation." He smiled. "Music happens to be my profession. So, like it or not, those who join in the resistance must agree to sing."

"Your name . . . Robert . . ." Amy said as they began down a decline. "Back at the museum, Mrs. Thembeka asked us if *Robert* had sent us."

"Winifred and I are old friends," Robert said.

From behind them, shouts rang out. Dan turned. The Tomas were flying out of the building, fanning out down the hill.

Amy panicked. "Hide the box!" she cried out.

"GO!" Mr. Bhekisisa yelled.

The group stayed close to one another, leaping over bushes, slogging through mud. Dan clutched the box. No time to hide it. No time to think.

They were totally outnumbered. "Dan," Amy said, running alongside him. "We have to give it to them!"

"Are you crazy?" Dan said.

"It's theirs, Dan!" Amy shot back. "We stole it! It's not like the other clues. We took it from them. That makes us just as bad as they are."

"Children, run!" Professor Bardsley cried.

Amy and Kurt took off at a sprint through the trees. Dan followed behind, looking left and right.

Mondli had said there were hunting traps. But what kind of traps? Iron jaws? Suspended cages? And where were they, anyway?

The map.

Dan stopped short and swung open his backpack. He reached inside and pulled out a rolled-up sheet of paper.

"Guys! *STOP RIGHT NOW!*"

Amy and Kurt spun around at the sound of Dan's voice. He was running toward them, his face red.

"Did we lose them?" Professor Bardsley asked.

"Just tell your people to stop!" Dan insisted.

Professor Bardsley shouted to the others, who began turning curiously.

Just ahead of them, visible through the trees, was a huge grassy clearing.

"We have to stay out of this clearing at all costs," Dan insisted, running past them until he was at the edges of the tree line.

The others gathered behind him, staring at the sun-drenched, oval field. "This may sound crazy," Dan continued, "but trust me. We have to go around to the other side."

The students, looking skeptical, wound their way around the clearing to the other side. They huddled behind bushes, shrouded by the canopies of trees.

"What's going on?" Amy asked.

Dan had that concentrated, intense look on his face, the one that in normal life said *I'm waiting to see if Mindy Bluhdorn will notice that I put gum in her hair* but now could mean anything.

"Everybody, listen!" Dan blurted out. "The Tomas are heading toward us from the left, the north, through the woods. Start making noise — now!"

"This is a strategy?" Professor Bardsley said.

"Just do it — please!" Dan said.

Amy looked at Nellie, whose face was ashen.

One by one, they reluctantly did as Dan said. Shouting, singing, beating trees with fallen branches.

Now Amy heard footsteps, voices. The Tomas were tromping through the woods. *"Dan, come on, we can't just stand here!"* Amy shouted.

The first Tomas broke through the trees. Among them was Mr. Malusi. Kurt stepped in front of Amy and began to nudge her back.

"Well, well," Mr. Malusi said, his face creasing into a tight, pained expression. "Daniel and Amy Cahill, I presume? I should have known. You didn't seem to be cut of the Holt cloth. You pulled off quite a trick. Now all you need do is return the box."

Soon the upper edge of the clearing was filled with kick boxers, sword fighters, and guards. The entire Tomas compound began edging toward Professor Bardsley's students, staying to the edge of the clearing.

"I don't believe this," Dan whispered. "This part isn't supposed to happen. . . ."

"What? Us dying?" Nellie said.

"Them staying to the edge like that, not coming into the clearing." Dan shouted over his shoulder, "Start singing! Spread out to the right and left!"

"Excuse me?" Professor Bardsley said.

"'I'm with you and you're with me'—that one!" Dan said. "We need to throw them off. To get them to move into the clearing!"

The students exchanged confused looks. But Kurt took a step forward, and in a voice deep and resonant, began singing:

"I'm with you and you're with me, and so we are all together, so we are all together, so we are all together. . . ."

The men and women crossed their arms over their chests, reaching for the hands of the singers on either side, to form a human chain. Their voices soared into the trees. As they sang, the stepped to the right in rhythm, along the perimeter of the clearing.

"Sing with me, I'll sing with you, and so we will sing together, as we march along! We are marching to Pretoria, Pretoria, Pretoria . . ."

The Tomas stopped in their tracks, looking uneasily at each other. Amy had no idea what on earth her brother had in mind, but she was singing, too.

"That's it," Dan said softly to Professor Bardsley. "Surround them on either side."

Bardsley looked at Dan as if he'd lost his mind. Then

a sudden smile crept across his face. "You are a student of Shaka. . . ."

Dan nodded. "The buffalo horns — some of us remain as the body, and the others . . ."

The students moved outward, into the trees, singing, enclosing the Tomas like a big fist.

Mr. Malusi looked to both sides with a smile that was half confusion, half amusement.

But the Tomas were angling their bodies, backing up, bunching . . . and slowly inching into the clearing.

"I am in no mood for a musical interlude," Mr. Malusi said. "And I am in no mood to attack stupid children. But you have seen the kind of training we do. And if you do not give me that box immediately, imagine what will happen!"

Professor Bardsley's people were closing in, arm in arm. All around Mr. Malusi, the Tomas were crowding in, waiting for orders.

Dan took a deep breath and held the box tight. "Over my dead body," he said.

Mr. Malusi shrugged. *All right, Tomas . . . ATTACK!*

CHAPTER 24

"YEEEEEEAAAAAAAAHHHGH!"

The voices caromed through the clearing, blood-thirsty and loud. Amy was shrieking behind him. The singing had stopped.

And then, nothing. No sound at all.

Dan could feel his arms shaking. His fingertips were numb around the box. But he was still holding it. Around the clearing, Professor Bardsley's students had gathered, all of them staring downward.

The Tomas were . . . gone.

There are traps.

Dan was shaking. "I — I don't believe it worked . . ." he murmured.

Where the grassy field had been was now a huge hole, at least ten feet deep and nearly the entire circumference of the clearing. From the bottom, among the throng of bruised and groaning Tomas heroes, Mr. Malusi lay dazed.

"Dan, what did you just do?" Amy was pulling him

from behind, shrieking.

Numbly, Dan pulled out the rolled-up map. "Mr. Mondli gave us this. It's a topographical map. It shows this humongous trap. I don't know what they catch in here. Maybe rhinos."

Professor Bardsley was wiping his brow with a handkerchief. "Brilliant, my boy. I don't know if we'd have made it without you!"

"Without Shaka," Dan corrected.

Move the body forward, then let the horns form outward to the side. Squeeze your enemy.

"The buffalo horn formation worked in battle," Dan went on. "People still use the technique in wars. These guys weren't going where we wanted them to. We needed to get them to move. I just thought we could . . . learn from history, I guess."

"Wait," Nellie said. "Is that Dan Cahill talking?"

The Tomas were lying below him in a vast pit, moaning, arguing, trying to scrabble up the nearly vertical sides. The students stood at the edge, singing another song in a foreign language with flowing harmonies. Professor Bardsley smiled. "French," he said. "'*Mon coeur se recommande à vous.*' Orlando di Lasso. One of your grandmother's favorites. And mine."

"The box, Dan," Amy hissed. *"Open the box!"*

Dan tried to yank the top off, but pieces of the cactuslike plant were still jammed into the crack.

"Let me try," Amy said, smacking the top. She pulled

it open and broken plant roots spilled out. But even more had grown into the box through the crack. The insides seemed like one solid-packed tin of plant root.

"Whoa," said Dan, "it's like tuna."

Kurt produced a pocketknife. "You may need this," he said.

Amy stabbed the knife into the roots, chipping them away. "There's something in here," she murmured.

"Yeah, pressed cactus," Dan said.

"Not cactus." Kurt smiled. "That is *umhlaba*, also known as *inhlaba,* a medicinal plant. You'd call it aloe. It helps with many ailments. It's fairly unique to this part of the world."

"Dan, look!" Amy was pulling out a delicate piece of jewelry, a bracelet with gems that caught the sunlight, reflecting it in sharp pinpoints of light. She dropped the box and let the piece hang so it could be fully seen.

A glittering arrangement spelled out SHAKA.

"May I?" Professor Bardsley held the bracelet up to the light. He pulled out a small knife from his pocket and scratched one of the stones. "Dear God, those are *diamonds*. Do you know how much this is worth?"

Dan reached out, running his fingers over the clear, cool stones. He recalled the words of the old man at the Shaka Museum in Durban:

Churchill was obsessed with Shaka. That is why he traveled to South Africa. Not to report. Not to fight. To find out about the isipho.

"Um, guys?" Dan said. "Do any of you know the word *isipho*?"

"A Zulu word," Professor Bardsley said. "It means *gift*."

Dan's brain was swirling. Churchill had been on a mission. He was obsessed with the Tomas Clue. He had been jailed, had hidden in a mine—and none of that had stopped him. As the men walked ahead, Dan murmured to Amy and Nellie, "In his note, Churchill said he wanted the thing that was *in the ground with Shaka*—and remember what the guy at the museum said? He was after the *isipho*! This is the Tomas clue, Amy!"

Diamond. The most magical of substances. Organic matter—plants, trees, animal remains—compressed by time and the earth's weight into the hardest, most brilliant substance known.

He held the bracelet to the sun, through the dappled cover of the trees. The diamonds had been hidden for who knew how long, and yet they shot back the sun's light with a radiance that was nearly blinding.

"We should have guessed," Amy said, taking back the bracelet. "Wars, apartheid—all of it happened because of the diamonds in the soil."

"Everyone wanted it, and people were willing to kill to get it . . ." Dan said. "Sounds like the secret to the thirty-nine clues."

"You will pay for this," Mr. Malusi's voice called out

from inside the pit. *"You are thieves of identity and thieves of our property!"*

Amy wanted to throw something at him. She counted to ten and unclenched her teeth, holding tight to the bracelet. Taking it from Malusi would be the perfect revenge. But she realized something: She wasn't sure if it rightfully belonged to the Tomas, but it sure wasn't hers, either.

Amy took a step forward. Kurt started to follow, but she motioned for him to stay and walked to the edge of the hole and looked down. "Um, about that shield you stole from the museum in Durban?"

Mr. Malusi glared at her silently.

"Maybe the Tomas still believe that one good turn deserves another," she continued softly.

The bracelet was beautiful, and valuable. But the hunt was about knowledge, not possession. She gave the bracelet a look, then tossed it down into the hole.

"Amy, what are you doing?" Dan shouted.

Nellie groaned. "That could have paid off my MasterCard!"

Below her, the Tomas began falling over each other, clawing to get to the priceless diamonds. Mr. Malusi quickly became engulfed in a sea of grasping arms. "Stop! *STOP — THAT IS AN ORDER!*" he shouted.

To the sounds of scrabbling and fighting, Amy turned her back and walked away.

CHAPTER 25

Karachi.

The name had been in Amy's mind for days, but it was now struggling for space against thoughts of an easy smile and a singing voice that gave her chills.

Back in Sydney, while threatening to feed Amy to sharks, Isabel Kabra had listed the places Dan and Amy had been. For some reason, she'd included a place they'd never visited: Karachi, Pakistan.

Amy had to accept that they were done in South Africa. Lingering any longer would be a mistake. The Holts were still out there, and angry. But that didn't make it any easier to leave.

"Let's keep in touch," Kurt had said before they'd parted. "I hope we meet again."

Amy hoped so, too. She couldn't expect it, though. She couldn't expect anything other than constant change.

"Flight 796, Johannesburg to Karachi, will be boarding in ten minutes," a voice echoed through the terminal.

"Hey, gotta go," Dan said.

Amy hugged Professor Bardsley. "Thanks for your help."

"Yeah, and the tunes you let me upload onto my iPod," Nellie said unenthusiastically. "Can't wait to listen to Renaissance church music."

"I suppose," Professor Bardsley said, "I cannot convince you to remain."

"Sorry," Amy said sadly. Professor Bardsley had been kind to them. He had driven the Yugo all the way back to Johannesburg, allowing Nellie, Dan, and Amy to sleep. He had found food for Saladin, helped book the flights, and even offered to pay. "We know how you feel about the thirty-nine clues, Professor Bardsley. But we have to continue. We were given a challenge, and we have to see it through."

"By grace," he murmured. His face crinkled, and he gave a small wink.

Amy wasn't expecting that response. "Grace . . . ?"

"She was a remarkable, lovely, generous woman," Professor Bardsley said.

"You *knew* her?" Amy said.

"Did she know *everyone* in South Africa?" Dan said.

Professor Bardsley nodded, smiling. "Grace had many friends here. Does this surprise you?"

Amy smiled. Bardsley had a long history with the 39 Clues and the Tomas. He knew Winifred Thembeka. Of course it made sense that he'd known Grace. "Let's stay in contact, Professor."

"Godspeed," he replied.

She, Dan, and Nellie turned to the security line. It

was quicker than they expected. After passing through the scanner, they followed the sign for the boarding gates, but a man with a mustache gestured toward a motor cart. "This way, please," he said.

"No, thanks," Amy replied. "We'll walk."

The man moved closer. "This way."

"Just give him some baksheesh and tell him to go away," Dan murmured.

"Wrong country, dude," Nellie said.

The man stepped quickly in Dan's path. In his right hand was a small knife.

"What the —?" Dan looked around frantically.

Behind him, Nellie drew in a breath. "Better do what he says. Now."

Amy trembled. She and Dan climbed into the back of the cart as Nellie took the front passenger seat. The man sped away from the gates, driving out a back door and across a tarmac. Small craft buzzed overhead and cargo carriers rolled by.

Soon they raced around the corner of a hangar. If the coast was clear, they could make a run for it.

Dan poked Amy. She eyed him and nodded ever so slightly. The driver swerved around the building.

Suddenly, Dan felt a bag come down over his head. *"Hey!"* he shouted.

Amy and Nellie were screaming. Dan tried to stand, but his arms were yanked behind him. He felt a coarse rope tightening around his wrists and a gag around his mouth.

In moments, he was being shoved from behind. They were walking on concrete. A rush of wind lifted his shirttail as a low-flying plane passed.

He felt himself being pushed through a door. Then two hands were shoving him downward, into a chair. On either side of him, he could hear Amy and Nellie grunting against the gags.

"One . . . two . . . three . . . all present." The voice felt like a scrape of acid down Dan's back. "Let's be civilized about this, shall we?"

The bag was pulled up over his head, and he was staring into the face of Isabel Kabra.

"Diamond," Isabel Kabra said, filing her fingernails and looking out of place in a molded plastic chair. "You came to South Africa and discovered the clue was diamond. Aren't they clever, children?"

"Hope it wasn't too . . . erm, *hard* for you," Natalie said, snickering.

"A pity you had to strain yourselves," Ian continued, "when we could have easily told you."

The mustached man squatted behind Amy, Dan, and Nellie, tying their legs to the chair. Isabel, Ian, and Natalie faced them across the cement floor of a storage shed. Shelves were crammed with cans, boxes, tools, and parts. Behind Ian's head was a huge, dented propeller lying sideways on a machine with a fan belt.

Amy pulled at her restraints. Isabel knew about the Clue. Somehow she'd tracked them down. But Amy was no longer surprised at Isabel. No longer scared. At this point, all she wanted to do was one thing.

Get her.

"How did you know? Dan sputtered. "This was a Tomas clue!"

"Churchill was a Lucian, dear," Isabel said with a chortle. "He found the Tomas clue a hundred years ago. Did you really think we wouldn't know?"

"Indeed," Ian piped up. "Well put, Mother."

She shot him a glance and he shut up.

"So . . . if you know it already," Nellie said, "why are we here?"

"I missed you, darlings," Isabel replied. "Ever since our awful little tête-à-tête with the sharks, Amy — for which I apologize — I've had a bit of a reawakening. I've been wondering about your health."

"You didn't seem too concerned about it when you set that fire, you animal!" Amy said.

Dan glared at her, his face rigid with fear.

But Isabel just shook her head sadly. "Animal. This is a strong word for someone who murdered Irina Spasky."

"Me — *murder?* — it was YOU!" Amy shouted.

"Really? Hmm, that's not what the newspapers are saying," Isabel said. "Are they, children?"

"Indeed," Ian said.

"Is that all you can say?" Isabel snapped, then turned

back to Dan and Amy. "You know, it is not easy being international fugitives. People tend to want you in jail. You wouldn't like it. Although I suppose it's in the genes. After all, Mr. and Mrs. Nudelman were masters."

Amy's stomach knotted. "Another lie!"

"Ah, the drama," Isabel said, smiling. "I see you recognize the name!"

"What do you want from us?" Amy demanded.

Isabel leaned forward. "I know how you feel about me, and I don't blame you. But I am in need of a few good young minds. And you, my dears, are in need of something more profound." She shrugged. "A family."

Dan looked at her in disbelief. "You want to *adopt* us?"

"Would you like a token of my good intentions?" Isabel reached into her bag and pulled out a vial of green liquid. "Voilà!"

"Your kids stole that from us!" Amy said. "In Paris!"

"And I am willing to share it with you," Isabel said. "You have no idea how important this is to the search for the thirty-nine clues. With it, you will be shoulder to shoulder with the winning team. Think about it. We will fold you into the Kabra family. You will lend your skills and knowledge to us. You will be like brother and sister to Ian and Natalie."

Natalie blanched. "Please! Distant poor cousins, perhaps . . ."

It took all Amy's strength to keep from laughing out loud. Isabel had something in mind—but if she was serious about *this,* she was truly insane.

She met Isabel's gaze. The eyes were like a lizard's, cold and bloodless. But for the first time — even as helpless as she was — Amy felt no fear. Fold into the Kabra family? She would rather die a hundred times.

"Amy?" Isabel said with a magnanimous smile. "I know, perhaps you need a moment to let this extraordinary opportunity sink in . . ."

Amy smiled back. "Actually, I don't need a moment," she said sweetly. "You can shove it."

Isabel recoiled. Nellie let out a hoot of laughter.

"Amy!" Dan cried out.

"So be it," Isabel snapped. "Some people just like to make things difficult." She held out the vial to her son. "Ian?"

Ian rose uncertainly. He placed the vial on a shelf just beyond the horizontal propeller. He paused for a moment, as if trying to decide something, then flicked a switch on the wall.

The propeller began to spin. It made a low humming sound that quickly grew into a roar. It was only about four feet off the ground, and the wind it created was strewing papers everywhere.

Isabel gestured toward the green vial. "One by one! Come and get it!" she trilled.

The mustached man grabbed the back of Dan's chair. He angled it toward the spinning propeller.

And he began to push.

CHAPTER 26

"NO-O-O-O!" Amy was shrieking from behind Dan.

Dan pulled at the ropes. The propeller was screaming in his ears, a silver blur, the blades coming closer. He smelled the burning motor, the grease.

Too tight.

Dan jerked his body, trying to tip the chair.

Ian Kabra looked queasily from Dan to the propeller.

Now the blade was inches from Dan's neck. He leaned back, eyes closed, his mind seeming to detach. He heard a scream and wasn't sure if it was his.

But he did feel his chair tilting. And his head hitting something, hard.

"Get him!" a voice commanded.

Isabel.

Dan opened his eyes. He saw Amy hurtling across the room, still tied to her chair, ramming her head into Isabel Kabra.

Suddenly, he felt himself rolling backward. "Dan! Dan, can you hear me?" a deep voice asked.

"Owwww . . ." Dan's hands were suddenly free. He

staggered to his feet. Across the room, Amy was on top of Isabel, pinning her to the floor.

A hand shoved him toward the door. "Go. We must not waste time. Make a left and head for Hangar Three. I will join you."

Professor Bardsley was pushing him. Three of his students wrestled with the Kabras while untying Nellie and Amy. The propeller was slowing.

Dan felt his neck, just to be sure. Then he ran to grab his sister. "Let's go!"

They raced to the door, with Nellie close behind. Isabel was shrieking, her voice piercing through the rumble of the slowing blade. *"THIS IS AN INJUSTICE!"*

As Amy and Natalie scurried out, Dan ducked back in to get Saladin. Then he ran around to the other side of the propeller and grabbed the vial of green liquid off the shelf.

Racing outside, he stuffed the vial into his pocket.

He caught up with Amy and Nellie just outside Hangar Three. The door was open, revealing a prop plane under a thick canvas.

"Are you okay?" Amy asked. "Oh, my God, Dan, I thought you were going to—" She swallowed the rest of the thought.

"What you did to Isabel was awesome," Dan said.

Professor Bardsley was sprinting toward them now. "Children, we are leaving," he said breathlessly. "You cannot stay in South Africa any longer. The Kabras can be subdued, but they will not be stopped. And there is someone else—" He glanced over his shoulder.

"Who?" Dan asked.

But Professor Bardsley ducked into the hangar, calling out, "Hall-oooooo!"

Two uniformed workers came running. "Do you have flight-path clearance, Professor?" one of them asked.

"Please get it for me—ASAP!" Professor Bardsley said.

The man ran off as the other worker helped Professor Bardsley unsheathe the plane.

Its sides were yellow, with red piping and a name in fancy script: *The Flying Lemur.*

"It's Grace's plane!" Amy exclaimed.

"Grace taught me to fly," Professor Bardsley said. "When she knew she was dying, she gave me permission to keep this old girl in business. Now, let's take her for a spin, shall we?"

Amy ran around to the other side and jumped into the passenger seat of the cockpit.

"Hey! I want to sit there," Dan protested.

"Dude, you weren't fast enough," Nellie added, sliding into the rear.

Professor Bardsley turned the ignition. The propellers spun. "Go!" the airport worker was shouting. "You have the green light!"

"They let you cut in front of everybody, just like that?" Nellie asked.

Professor Bardsley grinned. "Don't ask questions. Get in, Dan!"

Nellie pulled Dan into the backseat.

Dan plopped in beside her, fuming. "You guys think I'm not *fast enough*?" he said. "You think it had nothing to do with the fact that I'm holding Saladin, so maybe it was unfair for Amy to jump in like that?"

"*Mrrp*," said Saladin in agreement.

Nellie shrugged. "You could have done rock-paper-scissors for a half hour or so."

"Ha-ha. You just yuk it up with my sister." Dan folded his arms and sat back as Amy shrank in her seat.

"Dude, where are you taking us?" Nellie asked.

"If anything, he will be expecting us to land in Swaziland," Professor Bardsley said.

"He?" Nellie asked.

"*They*," Professor Bardsley quickly replied. "Anyone who may be on your tail. So I will take you to Mozambique. There you will board a plane to Germany, where I will arrange transport to — wherever it is you need to go next."

The plane rolled out of the hangar and taxied onto the runway, propellers whirring.

"Why are you doing this for us, Professor Bardsley?" Amy spoke up. "What's going on?"

"Because your work is done here," he replied. "Because you have found a clue. Because even though I am not a part of this, I respect that you are doing your grandmother's bidding."

"How well did you know Grace?" Amy pressed. "Did you know which branch she belonged to?"

As Professor Bardsley yanked back the throttle, the noise was deafening. *"What?"* he said.

The plane lurched forward.

"YEEE-HAH!" Nellie shouted.

From the backseat, Dan leaned into Amy. "You really think I'm so slow? Well, if I'm so slow, how come I was the one who remembered to hold on to this?"

He was shoving something in her face now. The Kabras' green vial.

"Dan, sit back and put your seat belt on!" Amy spun around. The vial was knocked out of Dan's hand. It flipped in the air twice. Dan flailed for it but only managed to bat it against the inner wall of the plane.

It smashed into pieces, spurting green ooze onto Dan's arm and the seat next to him.

"Auuuggghh!" Dan shrieked. *"Amy, I can't believe you did that, you idiot!"*

Amy sighed. "It's a *fake*, Dan."

But as a drop fell onto the seat, the fabric smoldered.

"UH, DAN?" Nellie shouted to be heard over the engine noise. *"WHAT DID YOU SAY THAT WAS?"*

Dan felt as if a zoofull of scorpions had dropped from the sky on his arm. *"OW,"* he cried out. *"IT STINGS!"*

The plane was in the air now. Amy looked at Professor Bardsley in the rearview mirror. "WHAT COLOR DID YOU SAY THAT SERUM WAS?" he asked.

"GREEN. OOZY. IT'S BURNING THE SEAT."

Professor Bardsley's eyes went wide. "IT IS NOT A

SERUM. IT IS A SLOW-ACTING POISON! THE KABRAS TRIED IT ON ONE OF MY COHORTS. IT WILL ERODE THE SKIN AND OVER TIME WORK ITS WAY INTO THE NERVOUS SYSTEM!" His hands were all over the controls now, flipping switches, setting dials. "I NEED SOMEONE TO MAN THE COCKPIT!"

Nellie leaned forward. "I WILL! I KNOW WHAT I'M DOING!"

Professor Bardsley quickly traded places with Nellie, causing Saladin to jump to the floor with a hiss. The old man reached behind the seat and pulled a canister labeled UMHLABA.

The pain was spreading. Dan felt his entire body vibrating. He gritted his teeth. *Don't think of it don't think of it don't think of it don't think of it . . .*

"WH-WHAT'S THAT?" he asked.

"CONCENTRATE OF ALOE," Professor Bardsley replied. "IT WILL SLOW THE POISON'S ACTION UNTIL WE GET TO A HOSPITAL IN MOZAMBIQUE. IT WILL TAKE ABOUT TWO HOURS, BUT YOU SHOULD BE ALL RIGHT. I BELIEVE THEY MAY HAVE THE PROPER ANTIDOTE THERE."

"*MAY* HAVE IT?" Amy was screaming. Her face was bone white. "YOU CAN'T LET THE KABRAS KILL HIM!"

Professor Bardsley nodded, his brows knitted.

He soaked a handkerchief and applied it to Dan's arm. It felt like ice water, soothing the fire. Dan's body began to settle, but there wasn't enough.

"MORE!" Dan yelled. "MORE!"

Professor Bardsley daubed the stuff more thickly.

"ISN'T THERE ANYTHING ELSE IN GRACE'S PLANE?" Amy shouted. "MAYBE SHE HAD SOME ANTIDOTE HERE!"

Bardsley suddenly looked up at Amy. "WHAT AM I TALKING ABOUT? I DO KNOW OF A PLACE WE CAN GET THE ANTIDOTE. BUT I'LL NEED TO RESET OUR COURSE TO MADAGASCAR!"

"ON IT, DUDE!" Nellie was flipping dials with confidence now. The plane veered to the right.

"Mrrp!" Saladin said, sliding across the floor.

"WHAT'S IN MADAGASCAR?" Amy yelled. Through Dan's fluttering eyelids, all he saw were the veins of her neck sticking out like tree roots. . . .

Professor Bardsley was now wrapping a tourniquet on Dan's arm. It felt good, but the pain was changing. It shot out in waves, up his neck, down to his legs, yo-yoing back and forth like some medieval torture.

Professor Bardsley's voice came to Dan like a radio station slowly fading. "WE ARE GOING," he replied, "TO YOUR GRANDMOTHER'S AFRICAN HOME!"

CHAPTER 27

"Dan . . . ?" Amy said, dragging her brother across the scrubby pathway, little more than a tangle of vines and roots. *"Dan, stay awake!"*

He was moaning. Deteriorating fast.

Amy barely noticed the entrance. Grace's "African home" was tiny, little more than a mound of rock and soil, a cave fitted with a custom-carved wooden door.

"We will not enter her working headquarters," Professor Bardsley said. "There is a small house around back, where she lived when she was here. I — I have a pass — a pass card. . . ."

Professor Bardsley was shaking. He'd landed the plane safely but taken a corner too sharp on the taxiing, clipping a wing. He was coming apart, Amy could tell.

Keep it together, she thought. *Keep my brother alive!*

Dan sagged between Nellie and Amy, no longer able to walk.

"You're g-g-going to be f-f-fine," Amy said.

Alone. The word muscled its way into Amy's brain.

For her whole life, she'd felt like a part, a half. It was never Amy. It was Dan and Amy. Like one word.

DanandAmy.

AmyandDan.

"Here we are!" she said, stopping before a small, shuttered shingle house as the professor fumbled with the lock. Dan was shivering again. His arms were wrapped in white tourniquets soaked in *umhlaba*, but his face was turning from red to yellow.

Nellie had her arms around him. "He's going into toxic shock," she said. "Hurry!"

With a loud *thwock*, Professor Bardsley opened the front door. "Sit him down!" he said. "I will go to the medicine cabinet."

Nellie and Amy wriggled Dan through the door.

Amy couldn't hold back a shiver of recognition. In a split-second view, she took in details that were hardwired into her memory — lace doilies on small dark-wood tea tables, demitasse cups placed as if Grace were about to emerge from the kitchen with tea, a portrait of Grace that Amy had drawn in third grade.

She and Nellie sat Dan down on a damask sofa. "*OWWW . . . OW OW OW OW!*" he cried.

Professor Bardsley ran in, a hypodermic needle in one hand. "You have to *inject* him?" Amy cried out.

"It is the only way to get it into his bloodstream fast," Professor Bardsley said.

Amy looked away, holding tight to Dan's hand. She

felt him stiffen briefly, a tiny whine emitting from his mouth that was more breath than sound.

Finally, she felt him go slack. Amy felt her heart turning inside out. "What's happening? Is he . . . ?"

Professor Bardsley wiped his brow. The knots in his forehead were deep. "We can only pray now."

"Thank you," Nellie said, "for everything."

Professor Bardsley smiled wanly. "Thank *you*. If I'd had to change the course of the plane myself . . ."

Dan's head lolled to one side. His mouth moved, but no sounds came out.

Professor Bardsley felt Dan's forehead. "I must return to the airfield for a moment. The way I landed *The Flying Lemur* may be a hazard to other craft. I will not be long. As soon as he is feeling well, we must leave. We cannot stay here."

Professor Bardsley was gone longer than Amy expected. Nellie continued to put fresh dressings of *umhlaba* on Dan's arm, but he wouldn't be back to normal for some time. The skin was badly burned.

"A-Amy?" Dan rasped, wincing. Amy ran to his side.

"Dan! You're speaking!"

"Duh," Dan said. "That Churchill note—the one Mrs. Thembeka gave us? Where is it?"

"Your back pocket, I think," Amy said.

"Want me to get it for you?" Nellie volunteered.

Dan groaned. "Could you . . . get me more dressing? Please?"

As Nellie disappeared into the bathroom, Amy continued exploring the room. She fought back tears. She had almost gotten Dan killed. Her anger had angered Isabel. Made Ian shove Dan toward the propeller. Then, in *The Flying Lemur,* she'd made Dan so frustrated he'd forgotten to be cautious about the poison. . . .

"Dan?" she said. "I'm sorry I've been a hothead."

Dan smiled weakly. "You're saving my life," he said. "So I don't care. Hey, check out the piano."

Tucked in the corner, barely fitting, was a spinet piano with a stack of sheet music on it. Amy stepped over to the piano and hit a few chords, but it was sadly out of tune. She remembered the hours Grace would spend in her mansion in Massachusetts, on a much nicer piano, teaching Dan and Amy all the words to her favorite Broadway showtunes. "Now, tell me the iPod compares to *this*!" Grace loved to say.

Nearby sat a desk whose ornately carved designs contrasted with the simple lines of the piano. Amy opened a drawer and jumped as a hairy spider crawled out. She looked over her shoulder, checking Dan. He was scribbling weakly on a pad of paper.

As Amy went to close the drawer, she noticed a small notebook tucked deeply inside. She pulled it out, rubbing her hands over the soft leather cover.

It was full of Grace's perfect, small handwriting, as

if Amy were opening a letter written yesterday. Each page was covered with notes—travelogues, mostly—with postcards from various countries taped to the pages.

Amy paused at a page of notes from a trip to China. Grace had never told them about this trip. . . .

I have writ ten Deng Xiaoping, who has agreed to grant visit to A & H when he discovered that they, like him, are M.

A & H—Amy's heart jumped. That would be Arthur and Hope! "Dan?" she called out.

"Amy . . . look!" Dan blurted out. He shuffled toward Amy, holding a sheet of paper in a shaky hand.

"Easy, Hercules," Nellie said.

Dan placed the Churchill note on the desk. "The letter . . . look what he wrote at the bottom."

"'The unbroken line shall deliver thy desire to the letter, if thou proceedeth downward ever, in single steps,'" Amy read aloud.

"Remember what we said about an unbroken line?" Dan said hoarsely "Look . . . Churchill's *circle*—one letter, a T. All the way at the top, all the way to the left! Now. 'Proceedeth downward in single steps'—that's what I couldn't figure out." Dan flinched as Nellie put gauze tape around the dressing. "What if . . . you go down . . . from that first letter. Step by step? Watch!"

11 May 1900

My Darling M____ C____,

    Tho' my loyalty to Britain &

1st taste for tumult may have drawn me
2nd to the Anglo-Boer conflict eventually, I
3rd commend you for urging that
4th my war reporting begin here now.
5th My loss in the election, as you say,
6th was a scar to be borne bravely &
7th is surely meant to strengthen me,
8th as will our army's troubles with the
9th mighty Boers strengthen it. Yes, I
10th did escape imprisonment from Pretoria's
11th State Model School, to where they'd
12th taken me (fortunately!) from H. Hill.
13th One cannot summon words for that
14th filthy pit in Johannesburg, a place
15th far more miserable than my fetid
16th hidey hole in Witbank's mines, post-
17th escape (where I was able indeed
18th to discover a realization, given herein!).

This I send you,
With all my heart,
Your Winnie

The unbroken line shall deliver
thy desire to the letter, if thou
proceedeth downward ever,
in single steps.

"'A realization . . . given herein,'" Dan said. "The realization was the clue, Amy. It was buried in this letter!"

"'Tomas clue is umhlaba,'" Amy read. "That's amazing!"

"Whoa!" Nellie shouted. "I thought the clue was *diamonds*! The Kabras said it was, too. You guys—you can't just reject that. There was that message about being 'in the ground with Shaka'!"

"What was *in* that box, Nellie?" Amy said. "What did we have to cut away? What was growing all over the place?"

"The clue we were looking for . . ." Dan said, gently touching his aloe dressing, "is saving my life!"

"Aloe . . ." Amy said. "It was right in front of our noses. The Kabras must not have decoded the Churchill letter. Maybe we're the first to do it!"

Nellie hooted. "Take that, Dragon Lady!"

Dan sank wearily in the sofa. "We're good, yo," he said, a peaceful smile spreading across his face. "Now all we need to do is figure out where to go next."

The house fell silent.

But Amy was fixated on the message in Grace's notebook. "Uh, Dan . . ." she said. "What do you think this means? 'I have written Deng Xiaoping, who has agreed to grant visit to A & H when he discovered that they, like him, are M.'"

"Deng—he was, like, the head of China, right?" Nellie said.

"A and H . . ." Dan said. "Arthur and Hope—Mom and Dad. They met the leader of China? Cool. Let's go there next."

"Maybe," Amy said. "But read it again—Deng agreed to meet them because he realized they were . . ."

"M," Nellie said. "What's M? Mandarin? Uh, wait . . ."

Dan stood and limped over toward a rear window.

"Where's Professor Bardsley, guys?"

He stubbed his toe on the foot of the piano and his knees buckled. Nellie ran to him as his hand landed hard on the piano keys. *"OW!"* he cried as an ugly sound echoed through the room.

Amy ran to him, still holding Grace's book. "Can't you sit still?"

"The book . . ." Dan was grimacing. "Read me some more . . ."

Amy flipped all the way to the end, where there were a dozen or so empty pages — pages Grace would have filled had she lived.

The last page of writing contained only one entry. "Listen to this," Amy said, reading aloud: "'I am feeling melancholy today, thinking about my dear A & H and missing them so. I cannot even bear to listen to my beloved di Lasso, because of the reminder . . .'"

"Reminder?" Nellie asked. "Reminder of what?"

Dan was staring at the piano, his face was ashen. "Oh, no . . ." he murmured.

Amy panicked. "Dan, sit! You are very, very sick!"

"Orlando di Lasso . . ." Dan murmured. "That's the guy Professor Bardsley specializes in. Loves the music and all. Look."

He lifted some sheet music from the piano and showed it to Amy and Nellie.

Amy glanced at the title, a complicated name in French. "That was the piece Professor Bardsley's guys sang after we defeated the Tomas, right?"

"He said Grace loved it," Nellie said.

"A *reminder*, guys," Dan said. "Grace wrote that his music was a reminder of something sad."

"Uh . . . I'm not following," Amy said.

"Amy, you want to know what branch we belong to?" Dan said. "Well, it would be the same one as Mom and Dad, right?"

"Yeah . . ."

"And they were M, Amy! They were able to see this Chinese leader because they were M. And Grace couldn't look at this music *because it made her think of them.*" Dan's face grew red, his raspy voice rising. "Did you read this cover sheet? Did you read this closely? Do you want to know who we are? Look at the third line!"

He held the music up to her face:

Mon coeur se recommande à vous
by Orlando di Lasso
A Madrigal, in Four Parts

Madrigal.

Amy blinked, gathering her senses, and closed Grace's book.

Placing it on the table, facedown, she noticed a photo had been laminated onto the back cover.

Arthur and Hope, looking young and happy, with their arms around a gaunt, unsmiling man.

From head to toe, he was dressed in black.

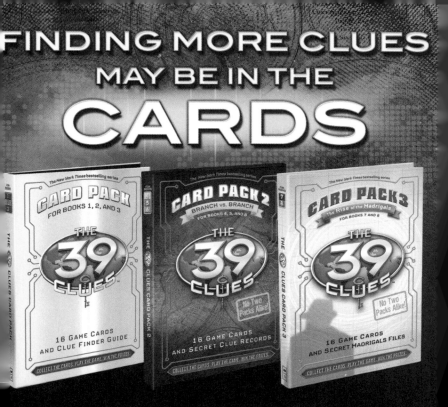

To: All Janus
From: Cora Wizard
Re: Clueless

My fellow Janus,
The other branches have nothing on us—no style, no wit,
no sense of how to run the world. Certainly they don't have
state-of-the-art strongholds underneath the canals of
Venice, Italy! But despite our best efforts, they are collecting
new Clues every day—OUR Clues. There is even a rumor that
the Tomas have a fresh lead on the Chinese legend.

Use your creativity. Everything we want is out there.
We just need to reach for it.

Cora Wizard

How to Start

1. Go to www.the39clues.com
2. Click on "Join Now" and choose a username and password.
3. Explore the Cahill world and track down Clues.

There are over $100,000 in prizes for lucky Clue hunters.

Read the Books. Collect the Cards. Play the Game. Win the Prizes.

JANUS